"BOWLING'S SENSITIVE and funny novel . . . demonstrates how negotiating others' discomfort can be one of the most challenging aspects of having a physical difference and how friendship can mitigate that discomfort. . . . [an] openhearted, empathic book.

—*Publishers Weekly*

"CONNOR'S TOURETTE'S SUPPORT-GROUP meetings and Aven's witty, increasingly honest discussions of the pros and cons of "lack of armage" give the book excellent educational potential. . . . its portrayal of characters with rarely depicted disabilities is informative, funny, and supportive."

—*Kirkus Reviews*

"A REMARKABLE, original story with true heart, a fresh voice, and an absolutely unforgettable hero. It's a book sure to give any reader goosebumps, teary eyes, and out-loud laughs. It's a book that doesn't just open your eyes, it opens your heart."

—Dan Gemeinhart, author of *The Honest Truth*

MOMENTOUS EVENTS IN THE LIFE OF A CACTUS

MOMENTOUS
EVENTS
IN THE LIFE OF A
CACTUS

DUSTI BOWLING

STERLING CHILDREN'S BOOKS
New York

STERLING CHILDREN'S BOOKS
New York

An Imprint of Sterling Publishing Co., Inc.
1166 Avenue of the Americas
New York, NY 10036

ISBN 978-1-4549-3329-8

Library of Congress Cataloging-in-Publication Data
Names: Bowling, Dusti, author.
Title: Momentous events in the life of a cactus / by Dusti Bowling.
Description: New York, NY : Sterling Children's Books, [2019] | Sequel to:
    Insignificant events in the life of a cactus. | Summary: After navigating
    middle school, Aven, born without arms, struggles with the challenges of
    high school, which test her confidence, strength, and sense of self. | cip
    verifier: please add sequel note to Insignificant events in the life of a cactus
Identifiers: LCCN 2019011133 | ISBN 9781454933298 (hardback)
Subjects: | CYAC: People with disabilities--Fiction. | High schools--
    Fiction. | Schools--Fiction. | Friendship--Fiction. | Self-confidence--
    Fiction. | BISAC: JUVENILE FICTION / Social Issues / Special Needs. |
    JUVENILEFICTION / Social Issues / Friendship. | JUVENILE FICTION /
    Family / Adoption. Classification: LCC PZ7.1.B6872 Mo 2019 | DDC [Fic]--dc23
LC record available at https://lccn.loc.gov_2019011133

Distributed in Canada by Sterling Publishing Co., Inc.
c/o Canadian Manda Group, 664 Annette Street
Toronto, Ontario M6S 2C8, Canada
Distributed in the United Kingdom by GMC Distribution Services
Castle Place, 166 High Street, Lewes, East Sussex BN7 1XU, England
Distributed in Australia by NewSouth Books
University of New South Wales, Sydney, NSW 2052, Australia

For information about custom editions, special sales, and premium and corporate purchases,
please contact Sterling Special Sales at 800-805-5489 or specialsales@sterlingpublishing.com.

Manufactured in Canada

Lot #:
2 4 6 8 10 9 7 5 3 1
07/19

sterlingpublishing.com

Cover design by Heather Kelly

FOR ADLAI,
WHOSE SUPERPOWERS INCLUDE
SMILES, SMARTS, AND STRENGTH

Moving on without you
Is not something I want to do.

—Kids From Alcatraz
(Punk band, est. 2018, Scottsdale, AZ)

ONCE, WHEN I WAS THIRTEEN YEARS old, my parents moved me from the land of flat, grassy prairies and towering, angry tornadoes and life-giving cool country air to the mysterious land of suffocating dust and prickly cactus and life-sucking desert heat to lord over a park of western-themed amusements that bring delight to many young children and a handful of immature grown-ups.

In other words, we moved from Kansas to Arizona to run a theme park, but it sounds much more exciting when I say it the other way, and I want you to think this is going to be an exciting story. What I mean is, it's absolutely going to be an exciting story. Prepare yourselves accordingly.

There were lots of changes. It was tough. The kids at my new school acted awkward around me. Things were looking dire. I didn't think I would be able to go on. I nearly gave up all hope until the day I met Connor, because he wouldn't stop barking at me. Connor became the best friend I ever had. Serious bonding occurred. *Serious* bonding. The kind of bonding that only happens when you pull the most epic steak prank of all time together. Trust me, it was epic and definitely not a complete and total fail, no matter what you may have heard or read.

Then we met Zion, and things got even better. Our trio was invincible. We were like Harry, Ron, and, Hermione—but with far less wizarding. And cloaks. Though cloaks would be amazing.

Connor was one third of us, a puzzle piece we needed to be complete—the bacon in our BLT (I was clearly the tomato since tomatoes are red and don't have arms and Zion was the lettuce since lettuce is all wilty). Connor was the third wheel in our tricycle, the third foot in our yard, the third bone in our ear. A BLT without bacon is vegetarian and not worth eating. A tricycle with only two wheels is a bicycle, and bicycles are a serious challenge for me. A yard can't be a yard with only two feet. A person can't hear with only two ear bones. It's science, people.

I tried not to think about Connor as I studied myself in the mirror over my dresser. I was wearing the new green tank top Mom bought me. It had a cute cactus pattern on it I liked, but I turned my head and gazed longingly at the sleeved shirts hanging in my closet.

Nope. It was still well over a hundred degrees outside, and I was not about to backslide after all that had happened last year. I would wear a green cactus tank top. I would wear it proudly, my head held high. And I would wear it on the first day of school.

I turned back to myself, my face full of determination. Which kind of made me look like I needed to use the bathroom. I relaxed my face a bit and did my best to seem blasé, which was like the coolest word ever and also how I was going to act about everything this year.

Oh, that kid passing me in the hall just put his hand up to high five me then burst out laughing with his friends? I'm so blasé I forgot about it the moment it happened.

Someone put a candy bracelet and Ring Pop on my desk? I'm so blasé I ate them both in one sitting during class and then fell into a deep sugar coma.

Oh, that kid just yelled, "Catch!" and threw a wadded up paper at me? I'm so blasé I reacted with lightning-quick reflexes and karate kicked that paper right back in his stupid face. Okay, maybe that reaction isn't exactly blasé. But it's awesome.

I continued giving myself my best blasé face in the mirror. No one could get to me. No one. If only my parents would let me tattoo up my nubs like this cool armless woman I knew online. They acted like I had asked to put skulls on each one when all I wanted were some flowers. Or tarantulas. Or some fearsome snake faces with lightning bolts for eyes and silver mercury dripping off their fangs like venom. Really, my parents were so unreasonable about it.

It didn't matter. I was going to school on my first day in my tank top, my armlessness on full display for everyone to see. And I didn't care at all anymore what anyone thought.

I was completely blasé.

If only Connor were here to do this with me. I hadn't anticipated this unexpected, hugely significant event. I always thought we'd be facing this together. I never imagined he'd leave. I never imagined he'd move thirty minutes across the city to a horrible place called *Chandler*, right on the cusp of starting high school, leaving me completely and totally and hopelessly and utterly alone.

Well, except I still had Zion and my parents and

my brand-new grandmother and Henry and Spaghetti (and a bunch of other way less cool animals) and all the people working at Stagecoach Pass including this girl named Trilby whose family ran the new smoothie place, but *still*. I never imagined Connor would not be in my life every day—only on a weekly basis, except when he's busy or I'm busy and we maybe only see each other every other week, or worse, every *three* weeks. I never imagined that would happen.

Then again, I never imagined I would make an earth-shattering DNA discovery, ride a horse with hundreds of people watching, stick it to the Man, and have a first kiss right at the start of high school. But you'd be surprised at all I'm capable of. Even without arms.

*I'm never going to fit in
But being different's not a sin.*

—The Square Pegs
(Punk band, est. 2003, Phoenix, AZ)

HIGH SCHOOL.

Two words that struck fear into the heart of every armless middle schooler I knew. Which was me. And, like, two people online.

Three thousand kids.

Three. Thousand.

And only seven hundred from my middle school.

No worries.

I totally had this.

Remember—blasé.

I entered the cafeteria, and the roar of high schoolers nearly deafened my ears. I searched for Zion among the chaos and found him alone at a table. No need to save a chair for me—people weren't exactly scrambling to sit with us.

"Finally," Zion said, though he couldn't have been waiting for longer than a minute. "I thought you would never get here."

"Just getting the kinks worked out in ceramics." I dropped my bag onto the table and eased my head out from under the strap. "I'm going to attempt the potter's wheel. It was the teacher's idea, but I think it'll be fun."

"I think it will be a huge mess," Zion said. "I'll have to sit here alone while you clean up every day."

I narrowed my eyes down at him. "For my first project, I'll make you a lovely vase for your room." I said *vase* the fancy way—*vahz*. "It will look beautiful displayed between the pile of dirty laundry and the brown banana peel."

Zion rolled his eyes at me as I sat down, slipped my foot out of a flip-flop, and opened the top of my bag with my toes. I had retired most of my flats by the end of summer break. Nothing like catching a waft of major foot stank while trying to put on some lip gloss to make you give up sweaty flats for good, dust or no dust. Now I carried foot wipes with me everywhere I went (okay, yes, they were technically butt wipes, but I used them for my feet, which automatically converted them to foot wipes).

Someone bumped into me a little bit from behind. I turned around and found Zion's older brother standing there. "Hey guys," he said with his big bright smile. Lando must have been the happiest guy on Earth— always smiling. I guess he had a lot to smile about.

"Hey," I said.

"Hey, bro," Zion said with his usual look of consternation. If Lando brightened up a place with his ever-present smile, then Zion consternated it up with his constant . . . consternating. Though Lando was only one year older than Zion, they were so different it was hard to tell they were brothers.

"How's everything going?" Lando pulled out a chair next to Zion. "How's your first day of high school?"

Zion took a loud bite of his apple and chewed like eating it required the effort of an aerobics class.

"Uh-oh." Lando scanned the cafeteria, an exaggerated fearsome look on his face. "Do I need to beat someone up?"

Zion and I both shook our heads. I knew Lando wasn't serious, but still . . . he was pretty protective of Zion. Except when they were the ones fighting. *Brothers*. I didn't get it.

"How's it going, Aven?" Lando said.

I shrugged as I dug around in my bag with my foot.

"Oh, fine. I mean, the faucets in the bathrooms are impossible to work, especially with no actual countertop for me to sit on, and I could live without the ridiculously shaped hand blowers I can't fit my feet down into." I finally found what I was searching for and pulled it out. I held it up in my toes. "Good thing I have foot sanitizer!"

Lando laughed and held out his hand. "Let me in on that." I squeezed some into his hands, which he rubbed together. Then he held them to his nose. "*Ah!*" he cried. "It smells all fruity."

"Yes, now you smell like a girl," I told him.

"You should have warned me."

I smiled innocently. "Sorry, *Lando-lina*. Would you like some of my lip gloss, too?"

"Pass," Lando said. "So everything else is going okay?"

"You don't have to worry about us," Zion said. "You can go sit with your friends."

"You sure?" Lando said. "It's your first day of high school, man."

"I'm sure. It's your first day of school, too." Zion motioned toward a table of cool kids. How did I know they were cool when it was only the first day of school? Trust me, you can tell. It was like they gave off a smell—like the kind a tarantula hawk gives off that alerts tarantulas to its presence. If I were the tarantula, then the cool kids were definitely the tarantula hawks giving off their strong *stay away from us or we'll sting you so we can use your paralyzed body to feed our babies* smell. Or something like that.

"All right," Lando said. "I'll catch you guys later." I watched as he sat down at the table next to a girl with perfectly shiny long brown hair. She wrapped her arms around him and hugged him, and I could hear her high-pitched squeals all the way across the noisy cafeteria.

I glanced around to see who was watching me as I pulled a granola bar out of my bag. Lots of kids. I tried with all my might not to care. Seriously, it was like the might of a hundred bodybuilders. Then my eyes stopped on this one boy. He raised an eyebrow and gave me a look I'd never seen before. It was a, "Hey there, lady," face straight out of one of the soap operas Josephine now watched since her life had turned into a parade of never-ending boredom over at the Golden Sunset Retirement Community. I turned away from soap-opera boy. Weird.

"What?" Zion said.

I shook my head. "Nothing." I glanced back at the boy. He was still staring at me. Even weirder was that I could tell he was one of the cool kids. I hoped he wasn't making fun of me in some bizarre way.

Zion followed my gaze. "What is it? Why is he looking at you?"

"I don't know. Do you know who he is?"

"Oh, you mean *Joshua Baker*?" Zion said. "That guy is the biggest jerk ever."

"How do you know him? Is he a freshman?"

"A sophomore. I remember when he was in eighth grade. He called me Lardon."

I thought for a moment. "I don't get it."

"Like *Zi-on*, but with *Lard* instead of *Zi*. Get it?"

"That's like the worst name ever. It's not even creative."

"Actually it kind of is," Zion said. "I Googled *lardon*, and it turns out it's a piece of pork fat used in a variety of cuisines to flavor savory foods and salads."

I frowned. "Exactly how many times did you Google it?"

Zion ignored me as he glared at Joshua's back. "Even Lando hates that guy. And Lando likes everyone." I didn't know Lando very well—whenever I was at Zion's house he was always out with friends or at football practice with friends or in his room talking on the phone. With friends. Dude had a lot of friends.

"Chili has started doing the funniest thing," I said, trying to move away from what was obviously a sore subject for Zion, but he kept glaring at Joshua's back. I cleared my throat. This was important information I was about to relay and it required his full attention.

He finally moved his eyes to me. "What's that?"

"She's started putting her head down to my foot to pet her. Isn't that the cutest?" He didn't seem nearly as impressed as I'd hoped. "Can you believe how smart she is?"

"Yeah, I know," Zion said. "She's a smart horse."

"She's a *genius* horse," I said. "She's the only horse I trust enough to make the jump."

Zion's eyes widened. "Did you do it?"

"Not yet. But soon. I feel it coming. Maybe next lesson." I gazed at a colorful poster of the food pyramid on a nearby wall. I didn't eat nearly enough vegetables. My personal food pyramid required its own ice cream space. "It's going to be amazing—like flying. I can't wait."

"And I can't wait to see you do it at the horse show. When is it again?"

"November."

"That's a relief. I was worried it was going to interfere with Comic Con. That would have been a serious catastrophe."

I slipped my other foot out of my flip-flop and worked on tearing the wrapper off my granola bar with my toes. "Comic what?"

"Comic Con," Zion said louder, like that would help me understand. "Down in Phoenix. It's for all the geeks, the dweebs, the comic book nerds. You know, the people like my parents."

I glanced at Lando's table. "I wouldn't be so quick to exclude the two of us from the dweeb group. What do you do there?"

"People dress up as their favorite characters and there's a bunch of comic book and movie stuff to check out and they have panels that discuss all kinds of important issues in the nerd world—like who's the best Ghostbuster and what exactly are the magic rules surrounding Gandalf's powers. My parents have been on panels before."

I'd gotten to know Zion's parents pretty well over the summer. And I had to say, anyone who would prepare an entire slide show on the positive attributes of Magneto was so far beyond nerdy that I never had any worries about fitting in with Zion's family. "When is it?"

"In a few weeks. You want to go? Please go. You have to go."

I shrugged. "Sure, I'll think about it."

"I'm sorry," Zion said. "I shouldn't have phrased that in any way as a request. As my friend, you are morally obligated to go. I already asked Connor, and he's going too."

"Cool," I said. "I'm sure it will be fun. Do I need to dress up?"

"Well, you don't have to, but a lot of people do. It's pretty much a requirement in my family so I guess you better come up with something. You can borrow one of our Darth Vader masks if you want."

"One of them? How many do you have?"

"I think like eight."

I grinned. "What else do you have?"

Zion took another bite of his apple and chewed thoughtfully. "I'll have to go through the costume closet and see what I can find for you."

"Whoa. Costume closet? How come I've never seen it?"

"Didn't know you were interested." Zion looked me over a moment.

"What?"

"I think we have a Kitty Pryde costume in there that might fit you."

I finally managed to tear open my granola bar and worked on peeling the wrapper down. "Who's that? Is she awesome? Because I'm only capable of dressing up as super-awesome characters."

"She's pretty cool."

"Well, what's her superpower?"

"Phasing."

I scowled and took a bite of my granola bar. "That sounds lame."

"No, it's a good superpower. Basically she can quantum-tunnel through solid matter."

I stared at Zion, slowly chewing my granola bar. I gulped. "I'm sorry, but did you say you *weren't* a geek?"

Zion pursed his lips. "Basically it means she can make parts of herself intangible so she can pass through things."

"Like the Invisible Man."

Zion exhaled with impatience. "No, the Invisible Man is *invisible*; he's not *intangible*. You can't see him, but he still has a regular body."

I mulled this over. "Would you rather be invisible or intangible?"

"Invisible," Zion said without hesitation. "What about you?"

"Probably invisible. Although, if I could make myself intangible I wouldn't have to deal with door handles anymore. What are you going as?"

"My ma's making me a Batman costume."

"I thought maybe you'd go as Morpheus." I snickered. "All bald and mysterious."

"My parents would love that," Zion said. "But no thanks."

I resisted the urge to look around again to see if people were watching me eat. I *knew* they were. There was no need to keep checking. Even though I'd gotten used to eating in my old middle school cafeteria, this was a whole new world with a lot more kids. I knew I'd eventually get used to it here, too, but it was still a struggle.

"You want to do a guitar lesson after school?" I asked. I'd been working with Zion and Connor for several months, but now it was mostly just Zion and me. Our little duo. Our *LT* without the *B*. Our lonely bicycle. I tried not to act too mopey about it.

"I was going to watch Lando's football practice. He wants me to try to get more involved and maybe try out next year. He says my size can be a good thing in football. Plus, you know, exercise." Zion winced.

"I'll watch too if you can give me a ride home afterward." It was still over a hundred degrees outside, and sitting on those metal bleachers in the afternoon sun sounded like torture. But it seemed like you should spend the afternoon of your first day of school with a friend.

I saw some girls from the soccer team enter the cafeteria. Unfortunately Jessica had gone to another high school, and she had been my closest friend on the team. We had a few phone calls over the summer, but those had stopped. I'd been through this before with other friends. I knew all too well how it went.

The girls from soccer didn't seem to notice me. Soccer was over, and we would all have to try out again in the spring. Plus, this was *high school*. Everything was different. There were serious politics at work here. At least that's what I'd heard.

I glanced over and saw that Joshua kid still watching me. He mouthed some words, and I turned my head. "What is it?" Zion asked me.

I didn't want to know.

Zion and I sat on the metal bleachers after school, but we may as well have been sitting on a barbecue. I didn't have a hat or sunblock, and I knew I would pay the price. A terrible sun-scorched price.

My phone buzzed in my bag. Now that I was a totally grown-up high schooler who, like, owned an entire theme park and all, my parents had finally allowed me to get a cell phone. I dug it out with my foot but didn't manage to reach it in time before the call ended.

Armless-girl problems.

I set my phone on the bleacher below me, called the number back with my toes, then placed the phone between my ear and shoulder with my foot. "I got your text," Mom said when she answered. "You need me to come pick you up in a couple of hours?"

"No, Zion's parents will drop me off after Lando's done with football practice."

"Great. That works out well anyway because I'm stuck with this annoying lease paperwork for the new jewelry shop. You know, Dad would be appalled to find out you're watching Man Smash."

Sweat dripped into my eye and stung. I was kind of appalled myself. "Well, soccer is out of season. Nothing I can do about it."

"Isn't there like baseball or bocce ball or bowling or anything else you could watch?"

Bowling would've been so nice. *Indoors.* "We're watching because Lando plays, and Zion might play eventually, too. So you'd better get used to it."

"Enjoy the man smashing then," she said. "Love you."

"Love you, too." I put my phone back in my bag. I shook my head and sweat flew on Zion.

"Gross!" he cried. "Keep your sweat to yourself. I have enough over here." It was true—he had a waterfall of sweat pouring off him. I looked down at my already pink legs. I pushed them against Zion, trying to get in some of his shade.

He squinted at our squished legs. "Why are you acting like a weirdo?"

"I wish my skin wasn't so pale. I'm going to fry. Lend me your arms."

"What for?"

"For shade. Hold your arms over me like an umbrella the whole time we sit here. Is that too much to ask?"

Zion removed the plaid button-down shirt he wore over his T-shirt and laid it over my legs like a blanket.

"Such a gentleman." I turned my attention back to the field. "So which position would you like to play?"

"Lando says offensive lineman would be the best position for my size. Plus, he said he would feel good knowing I was protecting him."

"He's a total jock, isn't he?" I said.

Zion looked offended. "No. Football's not even his favorite thing."

"What is, then?"

Zion folded his arms. "He's an artist, I'll have you know."

"What kind of artist?"

"He draws."

I scanned the field and found Lando. "What does he draw?"

Zion shrugged. "Just stuff."

"That's specific."

"He just draws all kinds of stuff. Sometimes he draws me."

I watched as Lando pulled off his helmet and squirted a water bottle over his short black hair then shook his head. I had no idea how they could wear all that gear and play football in this heat. I fully expected someone to topple over face down on the field at any moment. "What position does he play again?"

Zion rolled his eyes. "I told you already—quarterback. I know it's not soccer, but keep up."

I saw Joshua Baker run onto the field. "Hey, it's that guy—the one who was staring at me in the cafeteria."

Zion scowled. "Yeah. It's unfortunate we have to watch him if we ever want to watch Lando."

Joshua looked up and found Zion and me in the stands. He smiled and waved at us.

Zion grunted. "What. In. The?" he said.

"Maybe he's nice now," I said and smiled back down at him. He *was* cute.

"No," Zion said without hesitation. "That guy is the worst."

"You haven't seen him since seventh grade."

"Trust me, Aven. He's evil."

"Maybe—"

"Lardon!" Zion stood and threw his arms up. "He called me Lardon!"

"I'm sorry," I said, trying not to giggle at Zion's outburst. "That is really mean."

Zion sat back down, picked up the corner of his shirt that was protecting my legs, and wiped the sweat from his forehead. It flopped back down against my leg with a wet smack. "Gross!" I cried, laughing and cringing at the same time as it stuck to my leg.

"You want my shirt, you get my sweat. Especially if I have to sit here and watch you make moony eyes at my archnemesis."

"He is not your archnemesis. You haven't even seen him in over a year."

"A year isn't long enough for someone like that to change."

"Maybe he had a near-death experience and his life flashed before his eyes and he realized he was a big jerk and that forced him to reevaluate his priorities."

Zion squinted down at the field. "Unless it involved a brain transplant, I seriously doubt it."

Why do you have to grow up
Because you age?
Why do you have to grow up
When life turns the page?

−Llama Parade
(Punk band, est. 2015, Los Angeles, CA)

MR. AND MRS. HILL PICKED US UP after Lando's practice. Mrs. Hill looked amazing, as usual, in a Spock T-shirt that read "Trek Yourself Before You Wreck Yourself" and a blue sparkly headband that matched her blue leggings. Mrs. Hill had the best collection of headbands I'd ever seen.

"Aven's going with us to Comic Con," Zion announced from where we sat in the third row of the van on the way to Stagecoach Pass.

"Great!" Mrs. Hill exclaimed.

"What are you going to wear?" Mr. Hill eyed me seriously in the rearview mirror. "Choose wisely."

Lando turned around and grinned. "Choose wisely," he mimicked his dad. "Seriously, though—you better."

"I was thinking of lending her Ma's Kitty Pryde costume," Zion said. "I think it will fit her."

"That's a good idea, baby," Mrs. Hill said.

Zion sighed. "Ma, seriously, with the 'baby.'"

Mrs. Hill narrowed her eyes at Zion. "Oh, I see how it is. Gotten too good for my 'babies.'" She turned around and stared ahead at the windshield. "All right, then."

Lando leaned back over me and shook his fist at Zion. "Stop being mean to Ma or I'll kick your butt, *baby.*"

Zion glared at his brother. "I'd like to see you try," he grumbled.

Mrs. Hill turned to Mr. Hill and acted like she was trying to hock up a loogie at him. Then he did it back to her. Then Mrs. Hill got into it, hacking and grunting and humphing. I suddenly realized they were actually talking to each other. Like, *communicating.* What language were they speaking? German? Dutch?

I looked at Zion for answers. His eyes were bulging like they were about to burst out of his head. "That's not fair! You guys can't speak Klingon!" he cried. "I know you're talking about me!"

Mrs. Hill crossed her arms and grunted. "We can do whatever we please. It's not our fault you don't want to learn the romance languages."

"Klingon is not a romance language!" Zion said. "And neither is Elvish! French and Italian are the romance languages. I'll never be able to put Klingon and Elvish on my résumé!"

Lando and I looked at each other and cracked up. "I'll never be able to put Klingon and Elvish on my résumé," Lando mimicked him. "For what job? Pooper scooper?"

Zion turned his fury on his brother. "Shut up!" Then he reached across me and smacked Lando's arm. Lando reached over me and smacked Zion back. Then they were in a full-blown smack attack.

I pushed myself against my seat, trying to stay out of the line of fire. "Yeah, I'm still here," I told them from under their flying arms.

"Keep your hands to yourselves," Mrs. Hill ordered. "Stop torturing Aven."

The Hills dropped me off at the front entrance of Stagecoach Pass, and I decided to stop in to visit Trilby at the new smoothie place before I headed home. She often worked there with her parents in the late afternoons and on weekends. I figured the more friendly faces I got to see on my first day of high school, the better.

I pushed my way into Sonoran Smoothies and waited while Trilby's dad finished up with a customer. "Hi, Aven," he said to me after the customer left.

"Hi. Is Trilby around?"

"No, she's out with her mom. Do you want me to tell her you stopped by?"

"Yes, please." I read his T-shirt. "The Square Pegs?"

He smiled and stretched out his T-shirt. "Oh, yeah. That was my band."

"You were in a band?"

"Yeah." He sighed. "Before I had to grow up."

"Why can't you be in a band after you grow up?"

He scratched at his stubbly cheek. "That's a good question. I guess we all didn't have the time for it anymore."

"That stinks," I said.

His face grew serious. "It *does* stink."

"What kind of band was it?"

"Punk band."

"Cool," I said. "Did you guys ever make any albums?"

"Yep. You can still download our songs."

"I'll look for them," I told him. "I've never listened to punk before."

His eyes grew huge like what I said was shocking. "You must remedy that immediately."

"I will."

I left Sonoran Smoothies and made my way to the soda shop to visit Henry, opening the door with my chin and shoulder. "Hi, Aven. You want some ice cream?" Henry said from behind the counter.

"No, just ice water, please. Mom gets annoyed when I eat ice cream right before dinner." Which was *all the time*. Seriously, I had probably eaten hundreds of gallons of ice cream since moving to Stagecoach Pass. Possibly *thousands*.

Henry placed a plastic cup of ice water on one of the little metal bistro tables and dropped a straw into it. I sat down and sipped. "How can anyone go to school in this heat?" I said. "I wish I could hibernate until November."

"I don't think Joe would approve of that," Henry said.

"Joe's at the retirement center, Henry. Remember? My mom is Laura."

He rubbed at his head. "Right. Sorry." He sat down at the table with me. He leaned forward, his elbow on the metal table, still rubbing his temples.

"Are you feeling okay?"

He shrugged. "I feel foggy. And I'm tired. Always tired."

"Maybe it's this heat," I said. "You'll feel better when it cools down. I think we all will." I watched Henry as he stared down at the table. "Henry?"

He didn't seem to hear me. He'd been going in and out like this a lot. He would be here with me one minute, and the next minute, his mind was off somewhere else entirely. Sometimes he remembered who I was. Sometimes he mistook me for my mother. And sometimes he was so confused he couldn't remember my name at all. I never knew what to expect.

And then I realized I wouldn't know how to get in touch with his family if he got really sick or something happened to him. Did Josephine? Did my parents? He was getting more confused all the time. Older. Weaker.

"Henry, don't you have any family?"

He smiled a little down at the table, traced the metal flower design with his shaky finger, hummed something to himself. Eventually he looked up at me like he was just noticing I was there. "Hi," I said.

"Hi. Did you ask me something?"

"I asked if you have any family."

Henry shook his head slowly and continued tracing the flowers. "No. No, I don't."

"No brothers or sisters?"

"I suppose I could."

"You mean you can't remember?" I had a hard time believing he was so confused he couldn't even remember if he had any family at all. Denise, the woman who worked in the petting zoo, once told me he had trouble remembering recent things, but that he was better at remembering things from the past.

"No, it's not that." Henry tapped on the metal table, making a *tinging* sound.

"I don't understand then. What is it?"

"You *should* understand, Aven. You know, you and I have something in common."

"What's that?"

He stopped tracing the flowers. "We were both orphans."

Mom already had dinner on the table when I walked in the door so it was a good thing I didn't fill up on ice cream. I stared at the glass casserole dish of macaroni and cheese sitting on the table. I knew she would never make macaroni and cheese under normal circumstances.

"So, Sheebs, how was your first day as a high schooler?" Dad asked through a bite of cheesy goodness.

"Apparently Mom doesn't think it went well since she made *comfort* food for dinner." I eyed her suspiciously across our tiny kitchen table. "Why are you trying to comfort me, huh?"

She scoffed and flung her long dark hair over her shoulder. "I happen to enjoy macaroni and cheese, I'll have you know."

"No, you do not. You call it toddler food."

"It's a special day so I made you a special dinner." She waved a hand in the air. "That's all. I should not have to defend my dinner choices." She took a bite and made exaggerated pleasure sounds. "It's so delicious and sophisticated and not at all like toddler food. I elevate macaroni and cheese to a whole other level. I am a world class macaroni and cheese cooker."

"So school went well then?" Dad said.

"It went fine," I said. "Except for one thing."

"What's that?" Dad asked.

"How can anyone go to school when it's still over a hundred degrees outside?" I complained. "It should be mandatory that the temperature drop below ninety before we have to go back."

"The school has air conditioning," said Mom.

"But the bus doesn't have air conditioning," I said. "It's like riding in a toaster oven on wheels. And I have to walk outside from class to class. And the *outside* doesn't have air conditioning."

"That's only for a couple of minutes before you can get back inside," said Dad.

"A couple of minutes feels like hours when you're walking on the surface of the sun."

"I've heard the surface of the sun is cooler than the area around it," Dad said. "So it's probably not that bad. Maybe we could vacation there sometime."

"Yeah, when we need a break from this heat," I retorted.

Mom tapped her finger against her chin. "You could bring one of those miniature fans. Some of them even have little misters on them."

I frowned at her. "How am I supposed to hold one of those and walk to class at the same time? And how am I supposed to use one of those in public when I'm not eighty years old?" Lots of people at Golden Sunset had those.

Dad grinned at his macaroni and cheese. "Tell us something amazing that happened today."

I thought for a moment. "My granola bar seemed to have extra chocolate chips in it."

"Now that's something positive," said Mom.

"That's me," I said. "Always finding the positive. And I got to watch Lando's football practice with Zion. Too bad they also practice on the surface of the sun."

"Yes, I heard about your afterschool activities." Dad said *afterschool activities* like they were dirty words.

"You better get used to it. I'm probably going to be watching football a lot since Zion wants to play eventually."

Dad sighed. "I guess I can live with it then. Feels like soccer season is a million years away."

"Oh, and we're all going to Comic Con together in a few weeks. I think the ticket is like fifty dollars, so I will accept payment now, thank you very much."

Dad's mouth dropped open. "Fifty dollars to go look at a bunch of comic book stuff?"

"You don't just look at it," I said. "You dress up, too."

Dad gaped at me. "Do they give you your costume?"

"No."

"So you pay fifty dollars to wear your own costume and go look at a bunch of comic book stuff?"

"I'm sure we can figure out a way for you to *earn* the fifty dollars, Aven," Mom said. "There are plenty of chores to be done around here."

"Yeah, okay," I said. "You can't blame a girl for trying." I took a bite of my macaroni and cheese and swallowed. "So what are we doing to bring in more customers this fall besides the horse show? We should do something before that. What's next? Ideas? Go."

Mom laughed. "Straight to business. I think you'll make a great manager here in a few years."

"More like in a few days," Dad said.

"While I was restocking the fudge the other day, Henry mentioned that Stagecoach Pass used to have a bonfire to kick off the fall season every year," Mom said.

"Can't do that," Dad said. "Too dry. No burning."

"But the fire would be contained," Mom said.

"Laura," Dad said in his let-me-explain-this-to-you voice that made Mom look like she might launch her fork at him. "You're not even allowed to have indoor fires in your *own* fireplace in your *own* home, and I would say that's pretty contained. No burning at all. It hasn't rained in six months."

Mom glared at Dad as she continued tapping her fork on her plate. "We could use an alternative source of heat for our bonfire. It doesn't have to be wood burning."

Dad grinned. "Yeah, let's throw a space heater in the fire pit. That will be a lot of fun for people."

Mom lit up. "Yes, it will be a bon-space heater!"

"That will draw the crowds," Dad said. "It will only take four hours to melt a marshmallow."

"*Hm*," Mom said. "A bon-toaster oven then?"

I laughed. "Okay, forget the bonfire thing. Henry also mentioned something interesting to me today."

"What's that?" Mom asked.

"He said that he and I were both orphans."

Mom and Dad stopped their forks midway to their mouths. "Really?" Dad said. "Did he seem, you know, *with it* when he told you this?"

Mom frowned at Dad. "Ben, I don't think *with it* is the proper medical term."

"What then?" Dad asked. "Did he have all his marbles?"

Mom shook her head at him. "That's worse." She turned to me. "Did he seem clear when he told you this?"

"Not totally," I said. "He was a little confused. But he remembered that I was an orphan when he said it, so . . ."

"Josephine is his emergency contact," Dad said. "He doesn't have any family listed in his medical forms, and he's never mentioned anyone else before."

"Where did he come from?" I asked.

Dad shook his head. "I don't think anyone knows. I'm not even sure Henry knows."

"Well, I can certainly relate," I said. "I know how it feels to not know where you came from."

Mom reached over and tugged on my hair. "You know now."

"No, I don't. I mean, not totally. I don't know anything about my birth father."

"What is it you want to know about him?" Dad asked.

"I don't know. Did he work here at the park? Was a he a rodeo clown?"

Mom laughed. "I like that idea. Or maybe he was a stunt man who threw himself off the buildings."

"They never did that, Laura," Dad said.

"Yes, they did," she snapped back. "Josephine told me. They used to have a big mat they landed on until mice chewed it all up, and they had to throw it away."

"Maybe he fell into one of the holes," Dad raised an eyebrow at me, "and they accidentally threw him away with the mat."

I rolled my eyes at Dad, but couldn't help giggling. "All right, can we please get back to Henry?"

"Why the sudden interest in Henry's past, Sheebs?" Dad asked.

"He's getting weaker and more tired all time," I said. "I was wondering if there was anyone he'd want us to contact if something happened to him. You know, before he forgets everything."

"I guess only Josephine," Dad said.

I stared at my macaroni and cheese. "There has to be more."

Mom smiled at me. "I think you just need a new mystery to solve."

So much to do
If I'm going to defeat you.

—Screaming Ferret
(Punk band, est. 2011, Tucson, AZ)

I MADE MY FIRST BLOG POST AS A
high schooler that night before I went to bed.

So I've been in high school for twelve whole hours, and I've already discovered there's a ton I have to do to ensure I have the best first year of high school that ever was had by a high schooler. I'm sure there will be a million more goals to come because here are twenty after only the first day:

1.   Three thousand kids. I figure I can make friends with about 10 percent of them by the end of the year. Maybe even *fifteen* percent.

2.   Go to a school dance. I've never been to one because they always play the "Y.M.C.A."

3.   Come up with a way of handling the "Y.M.C.A." at the school dance. Do I do it with my feet? My ears? My eyebrows? Maybe I'll just go to the bathroom while it plays.

4.   New locker. It only took me about five months to master my last one, so I figure I can master my new one in no more than *four* months.

5.   Do not, I repeat, DO NOT, develop a crush on anyone. Crushes are rampant in high school but not for me. Bachelorette for life.

6.   Come up with a better blog name. I had to change the name of this blog back to *Aven's Random Thoughts*, which is like the worst name for a blog ever.

7.   Learn how to jump Chili so I can put on the greatest performance ever at the Stagecoach Pass Autumn Horse Spectacular! starring the death-defying Aven and Chili. Okay, that's not the actual name of

the show. *Some* people thought a more boring name would be better. Anyway, check the Stagecoach Pass website for details about the Autumn Horse Show and mark your calendars, people!

8.   Master the topknot. Mine looks more like a top-trashcan.

9.   Start a petition to put air conditioning on the buses. Because who wouldn't sign *that*? Also, if I manage to make this happen, I'll be well on my way to accomplishing goal #1.

10. Start a petition for outdoor misters as well. They should be standard in every single outdoor area in the entire city. No, they should be *the law*.

11. Write the Arizona State Senate about this mister situation.

12. Grow two more inches so I can reach *A1* on the vending machine. That's the button for Cheetos. It's a bonus that I'd also be able to reach *A2*. That's the button for Milk Duds. I don't, in fact, like Milk Duds, but I also don't like them taunting me.

13. Improve my makeup skills. Lip gloss is supposed to stay on the lips, Aven. On the lips.

14. Buy some pencils because, yeah . . . I just forgot.

15. Pick a costume for Comic Con. It must be the exact correct balance of fearsome and awesome.

16. Get my friends to stop hating people (especially cute boys) who maybe could become new friends; but I can't be friends with them because my friend hates them. This is called high school politics.

17. Branch out a little bit with my lunch food choices. Like, instead of smooth peanut butter with strawberry jelly, maybe try chunky peanut butter with grape jelly. Or I could get really wild and try almond butter with orange jelly.

18. Adjust to the new cafeteria.

19. Stop worrying about other people looking at me while I'm busy adjusting to the new cafeteria.

20. Be *much* more blasé.

One day you'll find
You can be old in your body
But not in your mind.

—We Are Librarians
(Punk band, est. 2009, New York, NY)

THE NEXT DAY AFTER SCHOOL,

I rode the bus to the Golden Sunset Retirement Community. I checked in at the front desk, where the nice receptionist always dropped the clipboard on the floor for me so I could sign my name. Then I made my way to the "leisure room," where old people could engage in all kinds of leisurely activities—mostly staring at windows, walls, TVs, and floors while drinking tea out of paper cups and eating crackers.

I found Josephine sitting in a blue plaid recliner, her feet up, reading a novel featuring a bare-chested man with golden locks that flowed in the wind like a fan was blowing on them. I slipped my foot out of my flip-flop and tilted the book so I could read the cover. "Fireman on Fire?" I asked Josephine, raising an eyebrow at her.

She shrugged. "It passes the time."

"He can't be an effective fireman if he doesn't have a shirt. Or if he's *on fire*. Plus, that hair is a hazard."

"He has a shirt," Josephine said. "But you're probably right about the hair."

I sat down on the couch next to her recliner. Josephine lowered her feet and set her embarrassing book on the side table where I noticed a random set of teeth were also lying.

"*Ew*," I said. "Someone lost their teeth again."

Josephine stood up and called out. "Whose teeth are these?"

A hunched woman in a long maroon dress hobbled over and grabbed the teeth. She stuck them in her mouth and walked off without saying a word.

Josephine sat back down as though nothing had happened. "So, how have your first couple of days of high school been?"

"Pretty good. I mean, okay. All right." I shrugged. "Not too bad."

Josephine raised an eyebrow at me.

"It's like starting all over again. There are about a billion kids who are seeing me for the first time."

"You'll handle it."

"Yes, I'll handle it. No problem." I nodded furiously. "I totally got this."

"How's Connor doing at his new school?"

"He didn't start until today. I'll talk to him later when I get home."

I felt someone staring at us and glanced over at a wrinkled man with a bald-topped head and glasses. He wore a short-sleeve, button-down shirt hanging out of saggy pants. And then there were the Bert and Ernie slippers—one Bert, one Ernie.

"Josephine," I whispered. "That man is staring at me."

Josephine glared at him, and he quickly turned his attention back to the game of chess he was playing with a man who may or may not have been asleep. "He wasn't starin' at you, honey. He was starin' at me."

I looked at him and found him already watching Josephine again. "Why is he staring at you?"

Josephine jerked her head in his direction and he quickly went back to his chess game again. "Stalker!" she yelled at him.

My mouth dropped open. "Josephine, you can't yell 'stalker' in the middle of a . . . of a . . . respectable retirement center." I glanced at her book lying on the table next to her. "Or maybe not so respectable."

"I can yell whatever I want," she snapped. "Inter-loper!" she cried.

I watched the poor guy's cheeks turn bright red as he stared at his slippers. "What has he done to you?" I asked her. "And what the heck is an interloper?"

She took a deep breath. "Wherever I am, I find him sitting not far away, starin' at me like that with those beady eyes. Stalker eyes!" she cried out again. "Plus, he eats the chess pieces."

I gawked at him. "What?" I watched as he literally picked up a piece from the chessboard and put it in his mouth.

What?

I got up and walked to him. I scanned the chessboard while he sat there chewing. Then I made my way back to Josephine and fell down on the couch. "Well, maybe if you guys didn't use fish crackers and fruit snacks for chess pieces, he wouldn't eat them. And what is this? Preschool? Can't you get better snacks?"

"What are we supposed to do?" Josephine cried. "They don't replace the lost game pieces in this dump."

I shushed her. "This place is definitely not a dump."

"A nicer place would have *all* the proper gaming

supplies. Anyway, it doesn't matter. He shouldn't be eating the chess pieces." She glared at him and raised her voice. "And he shouldn't be watching me with that predatory gleam in his eyes!"

"Don't you think you're being a little harsh? Maybe he wants to be your friend."

Josephine scoffed, "Men like that are only after one thing."

"Men like . . . who wear funny slippers?"

"He could attack me at any moment."

"I'm pretty sure I could knock him over with one toe."

"Man's a stalker."

"Yeah, well you'd know a little something about stalking, wouldn't you?"

She pushed the footrest down on the recliner with a dramatic clang and sat up. "And just what exactly do you mean by that?"

"Gee, I wonder." I watched the man as he pushed himself up from his seat at the chessboard and walked over to us at a sloth's pace, shuffling his feet. "He's coming over here," I whispered. Bert and Ernie inched closer and closer.

Josephine refused to make eye contact with him as he stood in front of us, shaking. "Good afternoon, Josephine," he said.

She grunted.

"Hi, I'm Aven," I told the man.

He smiled at me. "I'm Milford."

Josephine grunted again, arms crossed, suddenly interested in the flowery wallpaper.

"Have you lived here long?" I asked him.

"No, I moved in last week."

The poor guy seemed like he was about to fall over from trying to hold himself up, so I said, "Well, it was nice to meet you."

He looked at Josephine. "I'll see you at dinner, Josephine."

Josephine rolled her eyes at the wallpaper and puffed up her cheeks as she blew out a breath. "I'm sure you will, Milford."

"I hear we're having Steak Diane tonight," he said.

Josephine cut her eyes to him. "And just what is that supposed to mean?"

I cleared my throat. "I'm sure it will be quite delicious," I said. I watched Milford scuffle away. Then I turned to Josephine, who was glaring at Milford's back. "You don't have to be so mean to him."

"I am not about to let that man hornswoggle me."

"Okay, I totally don't know what that means, but it sounds inappropriate."

"I don't want him staring at me like that."

Joshua popped into my mind. "You know, a boy at school has been looking at me like that the last couple of days."

Her face brightened. "Really?"

"Aren't you appalled?" I said to her. "I mean, aren't you going to get angry?"

"About what? 'Cause a boy likes you? Do you like him?"

"Oh, so when Milford does it, he's an *innerlooper* trying to hornswoggle you, but when a boy does it to me, it's all exciting?"

"Yep, exactly. Is he cute?"

I tilted my head at her. "Yes. But Zion doesn't like him. He says he's a jerk."

"Oh, Zion's probably jealous."

"I don't think so. Zion and I aren't like that. He doesn't like me like that."

"All kinds of boys are going to like you."

"I seriously doubt it."

"Why? Why shouldn't boys like you? They liked your mother, too, and you're just like her."

"Except she had arms."

"Oh, is that what this is about? Well, a boy who can't see nothin' but that ain't the right boy for you."

I tilted my head. "Gee, you're so old and wise."

Josephine rolled her eyes.

"Do you think she and my birth father liked each other?"

"I doubt they hated each other."

I crossed my legs and smacked my purple flip-flop against my heel. "Did you ever find any, like, red squeaky noses or squirting flowers or abnormally large shoes in her room around the time she got pregnant with me?"

Josephine stared at me like *I* was wearing a red squeaky nose. "What?"

"Never mind."

Josephine squinted at me. "So when's the next lesson?"

"Tomorrow. After school."

"You do the jump yet?"

"No, but I have a feeling it's happening tomorrow." I continued flapping my flip-flop against my heel. "Yep, definitely tomorrow."

Josephine picked her book back up. "We'll see."

I waited until she got back to her place before I hit the book from the bottom with my foot causing it to pop out of her hands and onto the floor. "What do you mean, *we'll see*?"

She shrugged. "Everyone will understand if you're too chicken."

I slammed my foot down on the floor and pushed my shoulders back. "I am so not chicken!"

Josephine grinned like her silly little name-calling tactic might work on me. Darn it. It *had* worked. Now I was definitely doing that jump tomorrow.

Just then a lady with a poufy blonde wig and a disheveled polka-dot blouse walked up to us. "Have you seen my teeth?" she asked. "I think I left them on the side table here."

My mouth dropped open, but Josephine pointed at the woman in the maroon dress who was now sitting in a chair watching the television, which wasn't on. "I think Betty over there has them."

**What do you mean
You've met someone new?
She can't possibly know you
The way that I do.**

—Kids from Alcatraz

I PICKED UP A CRICKET WITH MY TOES
and dropped it in front of Fathead. She immediately
attacked it. I had found the poor tarantula near the
front entrance of Stagecoach Pass about a month ago.
She was missing two legs, and I imagined she had
lost them in a brutal fight-to-the-death with a vicious
scorpion. Tarantulas ate scorpions—another awesome
thing about them. Why was it awesome? I mean, have
you ever *seen* a scorpion?

Fathead hadn't seemed like she was doing too
well when I found her and didn't even try to run away
when I'd nudged her into a shoebox with my foot. I
had cleaned up the terrarium I found in the old shed,

and now I was running Aven's Tarantula Rehabilitation Center. I hoped Fathead would grow her legs back, but if not, she was welcome to stay at the ATRC as long as necessary. True, she was my only patient so far, but I was sure more would come once they heard about my luxurious amenities: crickets at every meal, climate control, live guitar music, and plenty of dirt to burrow in.

My cell phone rang on the bed—the call I'd been waiting for. I hit the answer button with my toes and then pressed the speaker button. "Aven's Tarantula Rehabilitation Center," I announced to my caller.

Connor barked. "How is Fathead?"

I watched as she devoured her cricket. "Hungry."

"Has she molted yet?"

"Not yet." Connor and I had been waiting for Fathead to molt because she might have new legs after that. "I think soon, though. She looks awfully molty."

"Probably not if she's hungry. Remember, their eating slows down a lot before they molt."

I knew Connor was using Fathead to avoid talking about the important issue of the day. "How was school?" I lay back on my bed and pushed my feet against the wall, which had lots of dusty footprints on it.

Connor barked. "How do you think?"

I tapped my feet against the wall. "I think it was probably better than *you* think."

"If you think it was a blazing dumpster fire of suck, then yes, you think it was better than I think."

"I'm sure it wasn't that bad."

"Someone already barked back at me."

"We knew that would happen. Did your teachers explain that you have Tourette's to the classes?"

"Yes."

"And?"

"They mostly all ignored it."

"See!"

"Also . . . I guess there was *one* thing that made it slightly better than a blazing dumpster fire of suck. A girl in my Algebra class also has Tourette's."

I swung my feet around and jumped up from my bed. "Get out! Did you talk to her?"

"Yeah, we talked after class. She's nice. Her tics aren't as bad as mine, but she's just . . . nice. We ate lunch together."

I sat back down on my bed, my excitement fading for some reason. "Yeah?"

"Yeah. Tomorrow she's going to introduce me to some of her friends."

I cleared my throat and walked over to my guitar in the corner. "That's so great." I swallowed as I plucked gently at one string with my toe. "I knew it would be okay. What's her name?"

"Amanda."

"What does she look like?"

Connor was quiet for a moment. "Why does that matter?"

I shook my head. "It doesn't. I don't know why I said that. What's up with your dad, by the way?"

The whole reason Connor had to move to Chandler was so he could reconnect with his dad, who had apparently come to his senses and realized he was losing his only child. His words, I guess. Why his dad couldn't have moved to this side of town, I didn't fully understand, but he said it would have made his commute to work too terrible.

"Nothing," Connor said. Connor hadn't been thrilled about the whole deal, to say the least. "He wants to take me out for dinner tonight to celebrate the first day of school. He's so clueless."

"I think you should go."

"It's hard enough eating in public with people who care about me."

"I think he does care about you or he wouldn't be trying so hard. Plus, it's nice to have someone to eat with while your mom's working. I'm glad you don't have to eat alone."

"Well, I'd rather eat alone. No, actually, I'd rather eat with you."

I smiled. "Or Amanda."

"Yes, or Amanda."

My smile fell. I hadn't expected him to agree with me. "Or Zion," I added.

"Yes, or Zion."

"Speaking of Zion, he said you're going to Comic Con with us in a few weeks."

"Yeah. Are you going to dress up?"

"Are *you* going to dress up?" I asked.

"I will if you will."

"Okay. But don't tell me what you're dressing up as. Let's surprise each other."

Connor barked. "Cool."

Mom walked in. "I'll call you tomorrow," I told Connor and hit the end button.

"How is Connor?" Mom asked, sitting on my bed.

I gently laid my guitar on the floor then pushed it over to the bed and sat down next to her. I plucked at the strings. "Okay, I guess."

"How are things going with his dad?"

I scowled down at my guitar. "Okay, I guess."

"Is something wrong?"

I softly played a couple of chords. "He made a new friend already."

Mom's face lit up. "That's wonderful."

"Yeah, it's wonderful," I said with far less enthusiasm than she had.

She chuckled and shook her head. She put her arm around me and squeezed my shoulders. "It *is* wonderful." She kissed the top of my head. "I'm sure he's nice."

"She."

Mom looked down at me and nodded slowly. "Oh. I see."

"And she has Tourette's. So I guess they have a lot in common."

"Aren't you happy he made a friend?"

"Of course, I am." Geez, I didn't know how to explain how I felt. Would I want Connor to be all alone? Of course not. Would I want him to be eating lunch by himself? No way. Would I want him to be friendless for all of high school? No. "I just wish his new friend were a boy. I know that seems stupid, but that's how I feel." I pounded a chord out. It sounded awful. "And I can't help how I feel."

"No friend will ever replace you, Aven."

I kept plucking away at my strings, making some terrible horror movie sounding music that matched my mood. "Yeah, I know."

Open your eyes.
Open your ears.
You need to see.
You need to hear.
—We Are Librarians

"HI, AVEN," JOSHUA BAKER SAID TO me at my locker as Zion pulled some books out of it. Zion helped get my books in and out when he could since it took me so long and was a major pain in the butt.

My stomach knotted up. "Um, hi?" Now he was talking to me? It was weird enough that he'd been giving me his soap opera faces for three days.

"Hi, Zion," Joshua said. "How you doing, man? I don't think I've seen you since middle school."

Zion stood up and faced him, his arms full of my books. Zion glared at Joshua like he was a rattlesnake. "Don't you mean Lardon?"

Joshua seemed confused. "What?"

"You usually call me Lardon."

Joshua grinned. "Man, no way. I would never say anything like that." He turned back to me. "Can I carry your bag for you, Aven?"

I said, "Sure," as Zion virtually ripped my bag off me with one hand, nearly dropping my books all over the place, and slung it around himself. "I'm carrying her bag." He dramatically stuffed my books into my bag and then gave Joshua and me a triumphant look.

Joshua smiled at me, which made his blue eyes crinkle up in a way that made my belly do a little flip-floppy thing. "Okay, then. Maybe next time."

"Maybe next time," I agreed.

"Maybe no time," Zion muttered as Joshua walked away. "I don't trust that guy. People that mean don't change."

I thought about Connor's dad. "Maybe they do." At least, I hoped so. And when it came to Joshua, I really hoped so because he was awfully cute. He had the bluest eyes ever. I wanted to stare at them for hours, trying to figure out their exact shade, but I wouldn't do that because I would probably scare him. And of all the girls in school, Joshua seemed to like *me*. I didn't think a boy had ever *liked* me, liked me before. It was all very exciting and mysterious. If only Zion would stop being his usual buzzkill self and let me relish the moment.

"I don't think I want to go to Comic Con as Kitty Pryde," I said to Zion as we walked to class. "I want to come up with my own thing."

"Well, you better come up with something fast then. Do you want to go to the mall on Monday after school to look for a costume? They should have the Halloween store open by now."

"That sounds good."

"You don't have a lesson on Monday?" Zion asked as we walked toward English class—the only class we had together.

"No, I have one today."

"You still going to do the jump?"

"Absolutely I am," I said as we entered the English classroom. I took in a deep breath of relief. It was always wonderful to feel the cool air conditioning after being outside for any amount of time.

"Can I come watch you?"

"No way," I said. "You have to wait for the show. It will be all the more climactic."

"It will be climactic today because it's your first time."

"No, the roar of applause will really enhance the experience."

"What if no one comes for the show?" Zion asked, dropping my bag onto my desk and pulling out my English textbook.

"Don't even say that!" I shrieked. "You'll curse it! Quickly, gallop around the room four times backward while rubbing your head and neighing like a horse."

Zion raised an eyebrow at me. "That removes a curse?"

"No, but it would be really fun to watch."

"Aven, go right," Bill, the trainer, told me after school. "Go right. Go right!"

Sweat dripped into my eyes, blurring my vision. My helmet felt like a glowing hot anvil sitting on top of my head. I pushed on Chili's side with my left leg and pulled to the right with my right leg. My stirrups were specially made with reins attached to them so I could steer Chili with my feet. "I'm trying," I told Bill. "Chili is being too stubborn." The horse was so darn hot underneath me that it made me think Chili was an appropriate name for her.

"It's not Chili." Bill removed his cowboy hat and wiped at his sweaty forehead. I would have loved to remove my helmet and do the same. "You have to be firmer with her." He placed the hat back on his head. "Push your left leg into her side. Use your strength."

I did as Bill instructed, but nothing happened. I think it must have been this heat. Neither Chili nor I could possibly be our best selves while we roasted in the searing sun.

"Firmer," Bill said. "You won't hurt her."

I dug my heel into Chili's side and she finally turned a little.

"Relax, Aven. Horses can sense when you're all wound up."

"I am relaxed!" I snapped.

Bill scratched at his sweaty gray beard, which was like a foot long. I briefly wondered if all that facial hair helped keep him cooler, kind of like how a dog's hair is supposed to help keep it cooler. Why did it feel like the sun was even hotter out here in the dusty arena?

"How are we supposed to get to the jump today if you can't even make Chili turn?" Bill said.

Sweat kept pouring down my face, stinging my eyes, and with my boots and helmet on, I couldn't wipe it away. I was starting to feel light headed, and I knew better than to attempt the jump when I might be dizzy. My heart sank. "It's not happening today," I said. "It's just too hot."

"Aven."

"It feels like the sun is literally two inches from my face." I narrowed my eyes down at Bill. "Two. Inches."

"That's impossible since it's ninety-three million miles away."

"I think the scientists had a bad measuring tape when they decided that. Based on how I feel at this very moment, I'm pretty sure it's two inches."

Bill grinned. "This is your first Arizona summer. You'll get used to it."

I gaped at him. "I feel like I'm going to pass out if I have to stay up on this horse. Then I will fall off. Then I will possibly die." All I wanted more than anything was a cold glass of water to pour over my head. "Do you want to be responsible for my death?" I asked Bill.

Bill shook his head. "I guess that's enough for today."

Mom and Dad had taken me to meet Chili at a ranch at the start of summer. She was a mix of pinto and quarter horse, which was nice because she was a bit shorter than the average horse—which equaled a shorter distance to fall.

I knew when we met her she was the horse for me. Maybe it was that we had the same eye color. Or maybe it was the cool spot on her side shaped like a cactus. Or maybe it was the fact that she'd peed all over Dad's shoes. Whatever it was, I felt an immediate connection—kind of like my connection to Spaghetti.

Chili had come to us already having been trained by

voice command, but Bill and I'd had to teach her a few extra commands she didn't know. She was getting good at the new voice commands, and I had to admit she was a smart horse. And I was smart for choosing her.

"Down," I ordered Chili, and she lay down on the ground so I could get off her by myself.

Bill unsnapped my helmet and removed it for me. He pushed my sweaty, matted hair back from my eyes and forehead. "We'll get it." He smiled. "Don't worry."

There were a lot of horse ranches within twenty miles of Stagecoach Pass, and Bill had come highly recommended. He owned his own horse-riding business in Cave Creek. Some of his horses were going to be in the horse show since Chili was our only horse, and Aven and Chili do not a horse show make. Several other ranches had signed up for the show once word got around about it. It was all voluntary; we couldn't afford to pay them. But it would be fun and they would get good advertising for their businesses by being in our show. At least I hoped so. I hoped people would come to watch.

After I helped Bill untack and brush Chili, I made my way through Stagecoach Pass. I enjoyed riding Chili. I mean, I would enjoy riding her a lot more if the air weren't made of fire, but I still liked spending time with her. And I'd do the jump. No problem. I still had time.

It didn't have to be today, even though I was a little disappointed it hadn't happened, especially since I'd now have to tell Josephine I hadn't done it after all.

I stopped to visit Spaghetti, which always cheered me up. But he just lay there, unmoving in this heat. He'd become less and less responsive to me all through the summer, and I hoped it was only the hot weather causing it. Maybe he'd perk up once it cooled down. I knew I would.

I could only sit there with him for about one minute before I felt like I was going to die from heatstroke. "Sorry, boy," I told him. "I can't take it anymore."

I made my way to Sonoran Smoothies and pushed through the door with my hip. I was happy to see Trilby there. Trilby was my age, but because she was homeschooled she had a more flexible schedule and could work the smoothie shop in the late afternoons and on weekends. My parents rented Trilby's family the space, so we really had nothing to do with it.

We had rented out several spaces at Stagecoach Pass since our art festival—we now had a southwest jewelry shop, a pottery shop, and a sand art gallery. We were still trying to get a more casual sandwich shop going, but in the meantime, it was strictly the steakhouse for meals.

"Hi, Aven," Trilby said when she saw me. I was so enraptured at the feel of the air conditioning I couldn't speak for a second. "You are red as a beet." She laughed. Trilby always said whatever was on her mind no matter what it was. I kind of liked that about her.

"That's because I've been riding Chili."

"A beet riding a chili," Trilby said and did a little goofy laugh like what she said was hilarious. When she was done cracking herself up, she asked me if I wanted my usual—peach, mango, pineapple.

"Do you mind digging in my purse?" I asked her. "I've got these riding boots on."

"Sure." Trilby bounded around the counter and pulled a few dollars out of my small cross-shoulder bag.

When she was done making the smoothie, she set it on one of the little colorful tables for me. I sat down and bent over it and sucked it down. It was like an ice cold, sweet, juicy rainbow in my mouth that immediately shot to my head. I sat back and whimpered from my brain freeze.

Trilby sat down at the table with me. "So how did it go?"

When my head stopped feeling like someone was digging a chopstick into it, I said, "Okay. She's getting better at the voice commands."

"That's so cool," she said. "I never knew horses could do voice commands like that." She grinned. "Like a big dog you can ride. Like a really, really big dog." She giggled again and ran a hand through her short blonde hair, streaked with green and blue highlights. She always had different color highlights in her hair. She also had a wild amount of freckles on her nose and wore colorful T-shirts with bands I'd never heard of on them. I could see why Zion had a crush on her, though he would never ever admit it.

"So how's high school going?" Trilby asked.

"Fine."

"Is everyone nice to you?"

"No one's been *mean* to me. I'd say so far so good."

"Have you made any new friends?" Trilby was home-schooled, so she was obviously curious about the goings on of high school.

"Not yet, but I will. High school is a whole new world. Yep, a lot of politics to figure out."

Her eyes widened. "What kind of politics? Fill me in."

"Just like who sits with who in the cafeteria and stupid stuff like that." I took another sip of my smoothie and swallowed.

"That sounds terrible," Trilby said. "I don't think I'd

do well in high school. I have a hard time conforming to the Man's expectations and following any kind of politics."

I didn't know who the man was that Trilby was talking about, but I assumed it was her dad, which was weird because her dad seemed pretty cool. "I agree," I said. "I'd like a simpler life."

"You sound like you should become a farmer. I hear that's a pretty simple life."

I thought about that a moment. "Maybe I *should* become a farmer."

"You could farm beets."

I smiled. "And chilies." I took another sip of smoothie. "How do you like being homeschooled?"

"I guess it's pretty cool. It doesn't take that long to get my schoolwork done every day, and then I have extra time to do my art and work here."

"What kind of art do you do?"

She waved a hand around the smoothie shop at the framed pictures. I got up to check them out. They were all of chickens, but, like, cool colorful abstract chickens. "You did all of these?"

"Yep, and they're for sale, too."

I sat back down at the table with her. "I might have to buy one for my room."

"I'll give you a good discount." We sat there quietly for a moment while I swigged down more of my smoothie. "Do you think you'll go to any school dances this year?" Trilby asked. "I always wanted to go to a school dance."

"I'd like to go to one, even though I don't really know how to dance," I said. "And I'm not sure what I'll do when they play the 'Y.M.C.A.'" Nostrils, maybe? "But yeah, I hope I get to go to one."

"I think it would be so much fun," Trilby said. "I mean, homecoming, prom, and all that. They probably play the sort of soulless, commercialized, manufactured, mainstream music the masses enjoy, but I'd still have fun."

Oh, man. I was pretty sure *I* listened to soulless, commercialized, manufactured, mainstream music. Whatever it was. "What kind of music do you like?" I asked her.

She pointed both fingers at her T-shirt that had a funny cartoon drawing on it and read *Screaming Ferret*. "Punk, baby!"

"I don't think I've ever listened to punk. Isn't that like old British stuff?"

"No way. There's tons of great newer punk."

"How'd you get into that? I mean being homeschooled and all."

"My parents raised me on it. There was never a time when punk wasn't blasting through our house and car."

"You know what? Your dad told me he was in a band before he had to grow up. I think he said it was a punk band."

"Heck yes it was! The Square Pegs."

"Your parents seem cool. Maybe you can write down some punk bands I could listen to."

"Heck yes I will! You'll love it, Aven. I can tell you're punk rock at heart."

I had no idea what made a person punk rock, but for some reason, it made me feel good to hear Trilby say it. "Really? I don't think I look very punk rock."

"Being punk rock isn't about how you look," she said. "It's about how you feel. It's about what you believe. It's about saying, 'I'm good the way I am,' and spitting in the face of the Man."

I frowned. "Your dad lets you do that?"

Trilby laughed. "You're so funny, Aven."

I smiled. "So how can you tell I'm punk rock then if it has nothing to do with the way you look?"

"I can just tell. I know you'd refuse to conform to the Man's expectations of you."

I stared at her a moment. I could tell she was giving me a serious education, even if it was a confusing one. "I'm sorry, but who is this man exactly?"

Trilby leaned in, her face serious. "If you're punk

rock." I nodded. "And I'm punk rock." I kept nodding. "Then the Man is everybody else."

I kept nodding like I understood, when I didn't understand at all.

"Hold on a sec." Trilby ran behind the counter, grabbed her cell phone and headphones, then ran back to the table. "Listen to this." She placed the headphones over my ears and tapped her phone screen several times. After a few seconds, an electric guitar was blasting in my ears, playing the coolest-sounding riff ever. And I didn't think I could listen to anything else ever again.

You're fading fast, friend.
Don't forget to say goodbye
If this is the end.

—Llama Parade

I WAS SO STINKING THRILLED WHEN the weekend came because Connor and Zion were coming over. It made me want to prancercise down the streets of Stagecoach Pass singing the song "Reunited," which was definitely not punk rock at all—neither the song nor the prancercising.

They both stood with me over Fathead. "She looks a little sluggish," Zion said. "Is she okay?'

"She's lounging," I said. "I mean, what would you do if you had to sit in a boring terrarium all day? You'd lounge. It's a life of leisure." I suddenly thought of Josephine at the retirement center.

"I guess," said Zion. "Do you think she'll live?"

I said, "Absolutely," at the same time that Connor said, "Probably not." I kicked his shoe. "Yes, she's going to live," I said. "Then I'm going to release her into the wild like they do with the panda bears. It will be quite the heartwarming event. Maybe we can stream it live on the Stagecoach Pass website."

"What panda bears?" Connor asked.

"The ones in China," I said. "Keep up."

"Will she be okay with two legs missing?" Zion asked.

"I'm hoping she'll molt and then she might have two new legs—two cute little baby legs."

Zion's eyes widened. "Cool. I didn't know they could grow back their legs."

"Oh my gosh!" I cried out, causing the boys to jump. "What if I molted one day and had two cute little baby arms afterward?"

Zion giggled, but Connor rolled his eyes at me and clucked his tongue, a new tic he'd developed over the summer. He picked up my guitar in the corner and started playing a couple of chords like I'd taught him. "Amanda plays the piano," he said, strumming the guitar.

My good mood instantly faded. "Oh, yeah?" I said as cheerfully as I could.

"Who's Amanda?" Zion asked.

Connor sat on my desk chair and kept strumming. "She's a girl at my new school."

"She has Tourette's, too," I told Zion.

"That's cool," Zion said. "Have you guys hung out?"

"Just at school," Connor said, blinking quickly a few times.

"You should invite her to come here with you next time you come over," I said.

"That's a good idea," Connor said. "I will."

Oh my gosh. Why did he keep agreeing with me about everything?

"I'm probably going to go to her house one day after school next week," Connor said.

"Why would you want to do that?" I mumbled, staring down at Fathead.

Connor stopped playing. "What?"

I whirled around and smiled. "Nothing. Hey, do you guys know who the Man is?"

They both stared at me blankly. "What man?" Connor said.

"You mean, *the* Man?" Zion asked.

"Yes, the Man."

"What man?" Connor asked again.

"Oh, yeah," Zion said. "My parents know the Man

all too well. That's why they went off and started their own comic book business. Because they couldn't deal with the Man anymore."

I nodded as I thought this over. I was even more confused now.

"Why are you asking, Aven?" Zion said.

"Trilby was talking about him."

With the mention of her name, Zion's lips got all quivery. "Trilby?" he said, his voice cracking.

Connor and I grinned at each other. "Yes," I said. "The lovely Trilby."

Zion pressed his lips together into a thin line. "Whatever," he muttered.

"Trilby's pretty cool," I said. "You know, her dad was in a punk band."

"Seriously?" Connor said.

"Yeah, they were called The Square Pegs. I've listened to them. Their music's great." I placed my phone on the floor and played them a song over the speaker. We all three sat there quietly, the boys bobbing their heads to the music. "Pretty good, huh?"

"I like it," Zion said. "I like the guitar."

"I know," I said. "It makes me want to start playing an electric one." I jumped up. "Oh, you guys have to hear this other punk band. They're called Llama Parade."

They both laughed. "I bet Spaghetti would like them," Connor said. "We should go play it for him."

"Okay," I said. "You want to get some ice cream first?"

"What about smoothies?" Zion asked.

It was funny how Zion had suddenly developed a blended kale obsession. "What *about* smoothies?" I asked him.

"I'd rather have a smoothie," he said. "It's healthier."

"Uh-huh."

"Fruit is healthier than ice cream," Zion insisted.

"You do know they put ice cream in the smoothies, right?" I said.

Zion scowled. "*Sorbet*."

"Same thing," I said. "And we have to pay for the smoothies, but we can get the ice cream for free."

"Why do we have to pay for the smoothies anyway?" Connor asked. He'd clearly gotten far too used to the VIP treatment at Stagecoach Pass.

"Because we're just the landlords of that place. We own the building but not the actual smoothies inside it."

"Well, can't you *lord* over them and make them give you free smoothies?" Connor snickered.

"No."

The three of us walked to the soda shop, but Zion made us stop at Sonoran Smoothies on the way so he could "see what their specials were today." Connor and I both gave each other knowing grins as Zion froze up and looked at his feet when Trilby popped up from behind the counter. "Hi guys!" she said with her usual enthusiasm, hair now streaked with red.

I nudged Zion forward with my shoulder. "Don't you want to get a kale smoothie?"

It was like Zion's voice, his entire human body, stopped working in Trilby's presence. He eventually shook his head, still staring at his feet.

"I've been listening to your dad's band," I told Trilby. "Their music is amazing."

"I know!" Trilby said.

"He never should have stopped playing."

Trilby's face grew serious. "I *know*."

"I played Llama Parade for the boys, too," I said. "We're going to go see if Spaghetti likes it."

"Of course, he will!" Trilby laughed. "Make sure you check out those other bands I mentioned."

"I will," I said. I turned to Zion, but he was in total no-eye-contact-with-anyone mode. "Well, we're going to get ice cream in the soda shop today. We just wanted to say hi."

"Hi!" she said.

We left Sonoran Smoothies and made our way to the soda shop. As we walked, I said to Zion, "Funny how you wanted to go in there so badly to get a smoothie and then didn't get one."

"Yeah," Connor said and barked. "We know you really wanted to have that 'smoothie.'"

Man, I was so jealous when Connor used air quotes. I would have to add "not being able to use air quotes" to my list of things that stink about not having arms. There was something special about using body language to be sarcastic.

Zion shoved Connor. "Shut up."

I grinned. "Seriously, though, I can see why you wanted a smoothie. I mean, the smoothies at Stage-coach Pass are the prettiest, *er*, I mean the most delicious."

Zion ran after me, chasing me to the front steps of the soda shop. "Base!" I cried.

Henry sat in one of the rocking chairs on the front porch. "Aren't you hot out here?" I asked him, walking up the steps.

He turned to me, his face filled with confusion. He didn't respond. "Henry?" I said.

He tilted his head a little. "Huh?"

I knelt down in front of his rocking chair. "Are you okay?"

He slowly nodded. "Uh-huh."

"Do you know who I am?"

His face contorted like the effort of thinking was too much. "Aven," he said slowly. "Aven Cavanaugh."

I stood back up and faced my friends. "Should we get him some help?" Zion asked.

Connor and Zion stayed with Henry. Mom was out running errands, so I went to find Dad, who was busy working in the office at the steakhouse. "Dad?"

He glanced up from the computer screen he'd been glaring at. "Hey. I thought Zion and Connor were here."

"They are. They're with Henry. He seems confused right now. Maybe you should come talk to him."

Dad came back to the soda shop with me, but Henry, Zion, and Connor were sitting in the rocking chairs while Henry told them a story that we caught the end of. "And that was how I saved that baby rabbit's life," Henry was saying.

"How'd you save a baby rabbit's life?" Dad asked.

Henry looked up at Dad, a mischievous twinkle in his eyes. "I beat that snake with a stick until it let it go. Boy, you don't want to hear the noises a baby rabbit makes when it's being squeezed to death." Henry shuddered. "I'll never forget."

"When was this, Henry?" Dad asked.

"Oh, when I was little."

Dad leaned down. "He seems okay now," he whispered to me.

"Was your family there with you?" I asked Henry.

"Oh, no." Henry shook his head. "I never had any family. That was in the orphanage."

Dad and I glanced at each other. "What orphanage was that?" Dad asked.

"Let's see." Henry seemed to think for a while. "That would've probably been Angel Guardian at that time."

"You were in more than one?" Dad asked.

"Oh, yeah," Henry said. "All over the place."

"Did you have any brothers or sisters there with you?" I asked him.

Henry shrugged. "Don't know. I don't remember anything but the orphanages."

Dad leaned in and whispered, "Come and get me if he starts losing it again."

I frowned at him. "You know Mom doesn't like it when you call it that."

"Okay, if he has another episode."

Dad left and I sat down in one of the rocking chairs. "What was it like in the orphanages?" I asked Henry.

Henry rocked gently and stared down at his hands. "Oh, it was okay. I imagine not as good as living with a family."

"Were they nice to you in there?" I asked. "I mean the people who took care of you."

Henry scowled. "I do remember one or two nuns fondly. There were some, though, who were mean as snakes." Henry shakily rubbed the top of one age-spotted hand. "I can still feel the smack of the wooden brush. I was given more thrashings than I can count." Henry shuddered. "I don't care to talk about those parts."

Connor, Zion, and I all looked at one another, not knowing how to respond to this. "Did you have friends?" Connor asked, blinking his eyes and shrugging his shoulders.

"Oh, yeah," Henry said. "Had some good friends. When you have hard times like that, it can make for some good friends. It's the only thing that helps you get through it."

"Do you still talk to them?" I asked.

Henry shook his head. "No. Lost touch years ago." Then his face brightened. "You all want some ice cream?"

The three of us followed Henry into the soda shop.

"That was weird," Connor whispered to me. "One second he was confused, and then he seemed to recognize me and started talking about old stuff." He clucked his tongue.

"Yeah, but I don't think he knows who I am," Zion said.

We went to the counter, but Henry went in the back through the swinging doors. When he didn't come out, I went back there to find him. He was in the closet staring at a shelf of paper towel rolls.

"What are you looking for, Henry?" I asked him.

His eyes scanned the paper towels. "I came in here for something, but now I can't remember."

"Maybe you should close the store and go rest. You don't seem like you feel very well today."

He nodded slowly. "Maybe you should go get Joe."

"Joe is at the retirement center," I told him. "Remember?"

Henry frowned and sat down on the step stool in the closet. "I can't remember much of anything these days."

I leaned down in front of him. "It's okay, Henry. Everything is going to be okay."

Don't let them blindfold you,
Force into your mind
Something that's not true.

—Kids from Alcatraz

"WHERE DOES HENRY LIVE?" ZION

asked over lunch at school on Monday.

"He lives in a little apartment above the soda shop," I said. "Like ours above the steakhouse. That way he doesn't have to drive anywhere, and Mom makes sure he always has what he needs and takes him to the doctor and all that."

"Why does Stagecoach Pass have those apartments?" Zion asked.

"Josephine told me when it was first built there was nothing else out there, and it was all dirt roads. It was too difficult for people to travel to Stagecoach Pass every day for work, so they lived there."

"Interesting."

"Of course, Henry and my family are the only ones who live there anymore."

"Why doesn't he retire?"

"He doesn't want to. It's what he's always done. And it makes him happy." I popped a grape in my mouth. "He's going to be okay."

"I hope so," Zion said, swigging down his chocolate milk, his face worried. "He was so confused."

"The doctor told Mom he has something called sundown syndrome."

"What's that?"

"As it gets later in the day, he gets more and more confused. I've definitely noticed it from time to time. He'll be doing okay in the morning and then by dinnertime, he's disoriented. It depends on the day. Sometimes he's confused all day."

Zion studied the table, a frown on his face while I chewed another grape. "Are we still on for the mall today?" I asked him. "I've *got* to find my costume."

"Yep. My mom's taking Lando and Janessa and you and me."

I looked over at Lando's table. Janessa was the one with long brown hair and perfect makeup who was always mooning over Lando. No smudged mascara for that girl.

I turned back to Zion. "I hope the Halloween store is open already."

"Ma called them. It is."

"Oh, good."

"So what'd you end up doing yesterday?"

I popped another grape into my mouth with my foot, always aware of the many turned heads in the cafeteria watching me. "I brushed Chili, spent time with Spaghetti, and lounged with Fathead."

Zion grinned. "You should have called Fathead 'Cocoa' or something. Then all your animals would have food names."

Darn it. Why didn't I think of that? It was too late now; Fathead was her name and would be forevermore.

Zion glared at something behind me, and I turned around to see what it was. Joshua walked toward us. I flipped back to Zion. "Oh my gosh." I put my leg down from the table and slipped my foot back into my flip-flop.

"Hi Aven," Joshua said. "You look nice today."

I glanced down at my black flip-flops, jean shorts, and llamacorn T-shirt. In case you're wondering what a llamacorn is, it's an animal that is half llama and half unicorn. So basically, it's the best animal ever. "Thanks?" I said.

Joshua sat down at the table with us. "What are you eating?"

"Grapes."

"I like grapes."

I nodded. "Interesting. We both like grapes."

Joshua smiled. "I think we probably have a lot in common." He had a great smile. Good teeth. Most boys my age were toothbrush-challenged, but I could tell Joshua wasn't. It was hard to imagine him saying mean things to anyone. He seemed so nice. Maybe Zion was exaggerating.

I touched my flip-flop to his Adidas shoe. "You like soccer?" I asked.

"Yes!" He beamed at me.

"Then we probably do have a lot in common." I glanced at Zion, who looked like he was about to hurl all over the lunch table. I wished he would stop acting like this and just be happy that a boy seemed to like me.

"You have any plans for after school?" Joshua asked.

I turned to Zion. He frowned and shook his head at me. "Zion and I are going to the mall."

Zion kicked me under the table, and I shot him a dirty look.

"Cool," Joshua said. "We might be going to the mall later, too. Maybe I'll see you there."

"Okay."

Zion glared at Joshua's back as he walked away. "What is his deal?"

I shrugged. "Maybe he doesn't have one. Maybe the deal is yours."

Zion narrowed his eyes at me. "Why'd you tell him what we're doing? It's none of his business."

"You know, people change," I said. "Maybe he's trying to make up for being a jerk before. Or maybe . . . you're not remembering very well."

Zion's mouth dropped open and then he pushed his lips together. I was pretty sure he was grinding his teeth. "Maybe you're not thinking very well," he said through his clenched teeth.

"Nope. My thinking is working just fine. As usual."

"I think you're thinking challenged right now. You're using poor judgment, as my dad says."

"Never," I said. "I'm a tremendous judge of people. That's why *we're* friends."

Zion's face relaxed a little. "I really do hope you're not wrong."

I'll be there for you
When it all falls apart.
I'll be there for you
When they break your heart.

—Kids from Alcatraz

ZION, LANDO, JANESSA, AND I WAITED
at the curb for Mrs. Hill. Janessa and Lando ignored
Zion and me as they flirted with each other, leaving us
free to mimic them by making silly giggling noises and
exaggerated moony eyes at each other.

Mrs. Hill pulled up, and Lando got into the front
seat and slammed the door. Janessa turned to me. "I
guess the three of us are stuck in the back. Evelyn, you
should sit in the middle since you don't need the arm
room. And you're waaaay smaller than Zion."

Zion gaped at Janessa. "The van has a third row."

Her face lit up. "Oh, cool. Then you guys can sit
in it."

I turned to Zion as Janessa got into the van, my mouth hung open. Zion's eyes were huge. "I can't believe she just said that, *Evelyn*," he whispered. "It would have been funny if it was a joke."

I stifled a laugh. "I know, but I don't think it was at all. She's pretty skilled, though—insulting us both at the same time."

Zion and I climbed in through the sliding door of the van and sat in the third row together.

Mrs. Hill turned to us from the driver seat. "Everyone ready to go?"

"Yup," I said. "Good thing I don't need any arm room."

Mrs. Hill raised an eyebrow, and Zion snorted beside me. Janessa let out a loud breath in front of us like simply being in our presence made her bored.

Mrs. Hill talked endlessly to us about her painstaking process of picking her Comic Con costume this year. "I am definitely not going to go as Wonder Woman," she said. "Everyone will be doing that."

"You could be Nubia again, Ma," Lando said.

"Wear the same costume two years in a row?" Mrs. Hill cried. "I want to do something new this year, something I haven't done before. That rules out Nubia, Vixen, Misty Knight, Monica Rambeau, Skyrocket, and just about every black female comic book character that exists."

"What about Amanda Waller?" Lando said.

Mrs. Hill snorted. "And wear a business suit? Plus, no powers. Guys have it easy. The number of male comic book characters compared to the number of female comic book characters is so unbalanced. And don't even get me started on the number of mainstream black female superheroes."

"You could go as Storm," I said.

"So predictable," Mrs. Hill said.

"Maybe you should do something really out of the ordinary," I said. "Like go as a female version of a male character. Like the Hulkess or something."

Lando cracked up. "Hulkess," he repeated.

"I like it," Mrs. Hill said. "There actually is a She-Hulk."

"Cool," I said. "She-Hulk."

Mrs. Hill smiled at me in the rearview mirror as we pulled into the parking garage at the mall. "Good idea."

"Yeah, good idea, *Evelyn*," Zion whispered to me, and we giggled.

We all separated once we got inside, Lando walking off holding Janessa's hand. "No making out!" Mrs. Hill called after them.

Lando turned around, his mouth hanging open. "Ma, *really*?"

She turned to Zion and me. "Meet me back here in the food court in two hours."

She didn't need to warn Zion and me not to make out as we went off together. We headed straight for the Halloween store. I walked over to a wall of masks as soon as we got in there. I slipped off my flip-flop and grabbed a particularly bloody face with my toes. Then I sat on the floor and lifted the mask over my head with my feet, adjusting the strap. " What do you think?" I asked Zion.

"That's gross," Zion said. "I don't want to be around that all day at Comic Con."

I stood up and hobbled toward Zion. "But don't you want to make out with me?" I said from under the mask in a screechy voice.

Zion laughed and pushed me gently back. "Heck, no. Get away from me."

"Come on, kiss me," I said, inching my face toward Zion's and making disgusting slurping noises. "Kiss me, hot stuff." Zion squealed and tried to get away from me as I ran after him down the aisle with the mask on, still making wet kissing noises.

"Aven?" I heard someone say and I spun around. Joshua was standing behind me in the aisle with a bunch of other kids from school. His friends all gawked at me like I was such a weirdo, but Joshua smiled. "What are you doing?"

I stared at him through the eye holes in the mask. "Nothing," I said. "Just torturing Zion." I sat down on the floor and pulled the mask off with my feet and set it aside. Then I stood back up, my cheeks a blazing fire of red, no doubt.

Zion stood next to me and glared at him. "It's none of your business what she's doing." As much as I wanted Zion to let things go with Joshua, I also felt a sense of pride at how much his confidence had grown in the last several months. He would have never spoken up to anyone like that last year.

Joshua smiled. "Look, man, can't we let bygones be bygones?"

Zion shook his head slowly, but I asked, "What are you doing at the mall, Joshua?"

"Just hanging out. Can I hang with you guys?"

Zion said, "No," and I said, "Sure," at the same time. "We're trying to find Comic Con costumes," I told Joshua.

"Cool," Joshua said. "Lando mentioned Comic Con at practice the other day. I remember your family's really into comic book stuff, Zion."

"Yeah," Zion said. "And I remember how you called me a fat fanboy freak."

Joshua glanced from me to Zion as a couple of his friends snorted. "No, I didn't," he insisted.

"Yes," Zion said. "You did."

"How do you even know it was me?" Joshua asked. "You're always staring at the ground."

That was sort of true.

"And your brother and I are on the football team together now, so we should try to get along."

We all stood there quietly for a moment until I said, "Maybe you can help me pick out a costume, Joshua."

His face lit up. "Yeah, I'd like that."

Joshua told his friends he was going to hang with us for a while, and we walked through the store together. I motioned my head toward a Supergirl costume. "Too silly?" I asked him.

"No, I think it would look great on you." Joshua removed the cape from the rack and placed it around my shoulders.

Zion kicked at a rubber baseboard on a nearby wall. "I want to leave," he said. "I've already got a costume. And it's almost time to go."

I checked the watch around my ankle and saw that we still had forty-five minutes left, but I didn't feel like arguing with Zion, especially when he was being so unreasonable.

Joshua walked with us back to the food court. Zion was quiet the whole time while Joshua and I talked about school. Clearly whatever had happened between Joshua and Zion was long over because Joshua was a totally different person. I couldn't imagine him doing the things Zion had said, and it made me wonder again if Zion wasn't exaggerating everything.

When we got to the food court, Zion and I sat down at a table while Joshua went to get a smoothie. "You better not actually like him," Zion said.

"He's nice," I said.

"Aven," Zion pleaded.

"And he's cute."

Zion groaned.

"You need to let this go. Everyone deserves a second chance."

Joshua walked back to us, two smoothies in his hands. "Here, I got one for you, too, Aven." He set it on the table in front of me and sat down.

"That's so nice. Thank you."

As I took a swig of my smoothie, Zion got up. "I can't deal with this. I'm going to the bathroom," he declared and left.

Joshua gave me a weak smile. "He's giving me a hard time."

"He doesn't make friends easily," I said. I saw Joshua's group walk into the food court. They watched us with sly looks as they sat down at a table nearby. "Do you want to go sit with your friends?" I said.

Joshua shook his head. "No, I want to sit with you."

I smiled a little. "Why?"

"Because I like you, Aven?"

"Really?"

"Yeah, why do you seem so surprised?"

"You just don't know me very well."

"I know enough," he said. And then he set his smoothie down on the table and leaned in toward me.

A million things ran through my mind in the split second as his face moved toward mine. Oh my gosh. What was he doing? Was he truly going to *kiss* me? Was I going to have my first kiss? Right here in front of all these people? Right here in the middle of the *food court*? Right in between Taco Bell and Cinnabon?

I wasn't prepared. I didn't know what to do. I didn't even know how to kiss. What if I accidentally licked his nose or drooled down my chin?

Was this how it worked in high school? "Hi. My name's Bob. Nice to meet you. Let's kiss."

What if I turned away? Did I want this boy I barely knew to be my first kiss? Would he and his friends think I was a jerk?

I mean, Joshua was really cute. And he was popular. And he was nice. But still, how was this happening like this?

Remember, Aven. You are cool. You are blasé.

It was no big deal. Was it? I mean, *was it*?

I closed my eyes and waited for Joshua's lips to touch mine.

But nothing happened.

I opened my eyes and saw Joshua watching me. He shook his head and called out to his friends, loud enough for everyone in the entire food court to hear. "I can't do it! It's too gross!"

Their table erupted into laughter as he got up and walked back to them. One of them slapped his hand and said, "You lose, man. You should've picked truth. You lose."

My heart pounded. Blood flooded into my ears. My vision blurred. I couldn't breathe.

What.

Was.

Happening?

All of the noises in the food court blended together

until I could barely hear anything. My body felt light, floaty. Like I wasn't there. Like it wasn't real. Just a dream. I wished it were a dream. That it wasn't real.

And then I was back there. And I knew it had happened. And when my vision focused and I could finally draw a breath, I saw Zion standing there, staring down at me, his mouth hung open, a horrified look on his face. "Aven?" he said softly.

I jumped up from the table so quickly that I knocked the chair over. I stumbled on rubbery legs as I ran out of the food court. All I heard as I pushed through the mall doors into the scorching heat of the day was the blood pounding in my ears and the distant voice of my friend calling after me.

I walked around the outside of the mall until I was dripping with sweat and so far away from the food court, I didn't think anyone could find me. I stepped back into a store and took my phone out of my shoulder bag. I struggled to hold it with my shaking foot and dropped it onto the ground. I turned it over with my toes and saw that the screen was now cracked. My eyes filled and then tears spilled onto the ground next to my cracked phone as I struggled to hit the "Mom" button. I told her I was sick and she needed to come get me.

My phone rang over and over as I waited for her.

Zion, every time. And then texts: "WHERE ARE YOU?" "ARE YOU OKAY?" "MY MOM IS WORRIED." "ARE YOU STILL AT THE MALL?"

I finally texted him back: "I'M FINE. MY MOM IS DRIVING ME HOME."

I stood there over my phone, tears falling onto the department store floor, the worst humiliation of my life weighing down on me like it might crush me to death.

I texted one last thing to Zion: "DON'T TELL ANYONE WHAT HAPPENED."

Suck, suck, suck.
Everything sucks.
And everywhere sucks.
And everyone sucks.
Suck, suck, suck.

—Screaming Ferret

I WENT TO BED AROUND SEVEN THAT night, too queasy to eat dinner. I lay there a long time, listening to the player piano belt out "The Entertainer" in the saloon below me. Eventually I couldn't take it anymore. I put in my ear buds and blasted some Screaming Ferret to drown out the noise—the noise of the player piano. The noise of my mind.

How could I ever go to school again? I couldn't. There was no way. I would have to be homeschooled like Trilby from now on. There was no other option. I would rather die than go back to school.

Around midnight, I got up from my bed and sat at my computer. I typed out a new blog post.

I guess I've been sort of lucky in my life. Most of the people I've known have been pretty nice. Even when they haven't known how to react to me or they've said something stupid or they've given me one of the looks, at least it wasn't out of meanness. Maybe fear. Maybe ignorance. But not usually meanness.

Sure, people have said mean things. People have made fun of me. People have been rude to me. But I never knew the degree to which people could be mean. And it turns out people can be meaner than I ever imagined.

So I guess I've been lucky that I made it all the way to fourteen without having to come face to face with this unbearable level of meanness. And I don't know what to do with this knowledge right now.

I've always liked to believe the best in people—that people can change. That there's good in everyone—or at least more good than bad in everyone. But I know now that I was wrong. It sucks to be wrong. And I don't ever want to be wrong about that again.

Then I deleted it.

Maybe I wasn't there
To catch you when you fell.
But I'm here now
To listen when you yell.

—Kids from Alcatraz

I TOLD MY PARENTS I WAS TOO SICK
to go to school the next day. And the day after that. And
the day after that. I didn't know how I could ever show
my face there again. Not after my Great Humiliation, a
truly momentous event in history. Like the American
Revolution. Or Nathan's Hot Dog Eating Contest. The
only thing I could muster the energy to do was stick
my ear buds in and attempt to drown out my horrible
thoughts with punk rock.

Mom knocked on my door that third day, then
walked in. "How are you feeling, honey?"

I moaned. "Terrible." I wondered how long they
would believe I was sick.

"I'm sorry I've been so busy working and haven't been able to spend more time with you while you've been feeling bad," she said.

"It's okay," I mumbled. I was glad my parents weren't around. I didn't want anyone around.

"Zion's here."

I sat up. "Why?"

"He brought you some of your work from school."

"Well, he should leave so I won't get him sick."

"He says he's not worried about getting sick. And you don't seem to have a fever or anything. I don't think you're contagious."

"You don't know that, Mom."

Zion peeked his head out from behind her. "Hi Aven," he said softly.

Mom left, and I swung my legs around onto the floor. Zion dropped a small stack of papers on my desk. He tapped gently on Fathead's terrarium, but Fathead ignored him. Then he sat down next to me on the bed.

I couldn't look at him. He didn't say anything. Finally he turned and hugged me.

Pity hug.

I was so ashamed. So humiliated. And there was nothing he could say or do that wouldn't make it worse. "I'm sorry," I said.

He let go of me. "Why are you sorry?"

I stared down at my feet. "I wouldn't listen to you. I should have trusted you."

"You just always want to believe the best about people."

"I should have hated him because of how he treated you. Like, how desperate could I be for someone to like me?"

"You're not desperate. And I can't imagine you hating anyone. Even though . . . "

"Even though what?"

"Yeah, you totally should have trusted me. That's what friends are for, right?"

I scowled at the floor. "You didn't tell anyone, did you?"

Zion shook his head. "No, I told my mom you were sick. She was worried about you. Lando was, too."

I cringed. Lando and Joshua were on the football team together. I wondered if the football team would find out—find out that some kids found me so disgusting, they would make a dare out of kissing me like it was the equivalent of eating a Madagascar hissing cockroach. My eyes filled with more tears.

"Aven," Zion said. "That guy is a special kind of terrible. Like I tried to tell you. And so are his friends. Forget about it. Everything's going to be okay."

"Forget about it," I repeated, the tears rolling down

my cheeks. "Like you've forgotten about being called Lardon." I shook my head. "No wonder you were so down on yourself last year."

Zion shrugged. "You'll get past it like I'm getting past it. It's been tough, though. I didn't think as much about my weight in elementary school. I mean, I've always been bullied, but when I got to middle school it was like a whole new level with Joshua and his friends. I didn't want to see him do the same things to you. That's why I tried to warn you."

I flinched.

You should have trusted me.

I tried to tell you.

I tried to warn you.

I could see Zion was hurt. And I was hurt. I just hoped our friendship wasn't hurt.

"You're not . . . mad at me, are you?" I said.

Zion got back up and walked to Fathead's terrarium. "No." But he'd hesitated. And he hadn't looked at me. "Of course not."

"I know I should have trusted you," I said. "I'll never not trust you again. And I'm trusting you, and only you, to never ever tell anyone about what happened."

Zion turned around. "Of course I won't. Why would I?"

"I didn't think you would."

"Then why'd you say that?"

I shrugged. "I just want you to know I trust you."

Zion tapped on Fathead's terrarium one more time, but she didn't budge. "Anyway, I can't stay," he said. "Ma's waiting out in the car."

I was torn between wanting him to stay and make sure we were okay and wanting him to leave so I wouldn't have to deal with this anymore. I motioned toward the stack of papers with my head. "Thanks for bringing me my work."

Zion smiled. "That's what friends are for, right?"

I did my best to match his smile. "That and a lot of other things."

I walked Zion out then helped Mom set the table for dinner.

"You feeling any better, Sheebs?" Dad asked once we were all sitting down together.

I sat down across from him. "Not really."

"What's still wrong? Stomachache?"

"Yeah, stomachache, headache, throat ache . . . foot ache."

Dad tilted his head at me. "That's a lot of aches. I'm sorry you feel so bad." He fiddled with his fork a moment. "Are you sure this isn't about something else?"

"Like what?"

"Are you afraid to go to school for some reason?"

"No," I lied. "I mean, it's true I don't want to go anymore, but I'm not afraid. I just think maybe I would like to never to go to school again and possibly become a hermit. That's all."

Dad smiled. "I don't think you'd make a very good hermit. You'd get lonely."

"No, I could do it. I found an entire how-to article complete with steps, tips, and pictures. It didn't seem hard at all."

Mom tossed a potholder onto the table. "Really?"

"What were the pictures of?" Dad asked.

"You know," I said. "Just people . . . hermiting."

Mom placed a pot of Swedish meatballs on top of the potholder. "What were the tips?"

I shrugged. "I don't remember all of them, but one was to connect with other hermits."

"That seems . . . contradictory," Dad said.

I nodded. "Yeah, it wasn't a very good article."

Mom sat down at the table. "Why are you Googling how to become a hermit, Aven?"

"Just curious."

"Wouldn't you miss us?" Dad said.

"Oh, I'd still have to see you every now and then."

"Then you wouldn't be a real hermit," Mom said.

"Then I guess I'd like to become a part-time hermit. So if you never make me go back to high school again, I can accomplish my goal of becoming a part-time hermit."

"What has happened that makes you want so badly to never go back to school again?" Mom asked.

"Nothing," I insisted. "Like I've already told you a hundred times." I didn't realize how mean my tone had been until I looked up from my plate and saw the hurt in Mom's face.

I stared back down at the table. "Sorry," I muttered. I took the spoon from the pot with my foot and placed a sad lonely meatball on my plate. I stabbed it with my fork and chewed. I wasn't hungry.

I knew they were sitting there, not eating, staring at me. Waiting for me to say something else. But I didn't.

"We wish you would tell us what's going on with you," Dad finally said.

But I could never tell them about my Great Humiliation. I could never tell anyone. And I hoped Zion wouldn't either.

13

I WAS SO GLAD WHEN SATURDAY came because I didn't have to pretend to be sick anymore. Not only was I already behind on my work after missing four days of school, but I had also missed a riding lesson. What did it matter? I would never be good enough in time for the show. I would never be good enough . . . ever.

I finally left my cave of despair and wandered through the dead park; it was still too hot for many customers. I walked past Sonoran Smoothies without a glance. Would I ever be able to drink another smoothie again without thinking of what Joshua and his friends had done to me? Great. Not only had Joshua ruined high school for me, he'd ruined smoothies. And my phone. And possibly my friendship with Zion. And just my whole life.

Trilby burst through the doors. "Hey, Aven!" she cried.

I summoned the best smile I could. "Hi, Trilby."

"You want to come in?"

I shook my head. "No, I don't have any money."

"I heard you've been sick. I'll treat you."

Man, I wished so bad I were homeschooled like sweet, innocent, naïve Trilby. She had no clue how tough life could be. "No, thank you," I said. "I think I'm allergic to smoothies."

She raised an eyebrow. "Allergic . . . to all smoothies?"

"Yeah."

"Are you allergic to chicken smoothies?"

"That's not a thing."

"It could be. I could blend up some chicken and make a smoothie out of it."

"Gross."

"Not that I would *ever* do that. I would never eat a chicken, much less grind one up in a blender."

"I repeat: gross."

"Maybe it's the pineapple," she said. "Some people are allergic to pineapple. I could make you one without it."

"I told you I don't want a stupid smoothie," I snapped, and her smile fell. "I'm sorry. I still don't feel too well. I'm going to check on Spaghetti."

I left Trilby standing in front of Sonoran Smoothies, a look of confusion on her face.

But Spaghetti had no comfort to offer me. And I worried about him every time I saw him these days, which only made me feel worse.

I made my way across Main Street and stepped through the doors of the soda shop. I walked along the wall, scanning the framed tarantula pictures my birth mother had taken. "Hey, little Aven," Henry called to me from behind the counter.

"If I ask for mint chip today, Henry, are you going to give it to me or are you going to give me strawberry?"

He smiled and shook his head. "You want strawberry?"

I took in an impatient breath. "No, I want mint chip. Repeat after me. Mint. Chip."

Henry stared at me. "Mint. Chip."

"I don't want vanilla or chocolate or strawberry. I want mint chip." In the back of my mind I knew how snippy I was being. First with Trilby and now with Henry. But sometimes a girl doesn't want what she doesn't want and wants what she wants, and I wanted the comfort of mint chip right now.

I watched as Henry took the ice cream scoop. He opened the freezer and I cried out, "Mint chip!"

He jumped a little. "Okay, okay," he said.

I watched with satisfaction as he scooped some mint chip into a bowl. He came around and set it on the table for me.

I sat down in front of my ice cream and slipped a foot out of my flip-flop. I grabbed the spoon with my toes and shoved a big bite into my mouth, letting it melt slowly, freezing my teeth and making them hurt.

I felt like crying. Mint chip couldn't fix this.

Henry sat down across from me at the little metal bistro table. "Did you wake up on the wrong side of the bed this morning?" he asked.

I realized I probably did look like I'd just gotten out of bed. I hadn't bothered to brush my hair in several days, much less wash it. I probably stunk, too.

I didn't want to talk about myself. "Tell me more about the orphanage, Henry."

"Orphanage?"

"Yeah. You know, how you were an orphan, like me?"

"You're no orphan."

"I was," I said.

He shook his head. "I know your mama. You're no orphan."

"My mama's dead," I said.

Henry's mouth dropped open. "Joe . . . Joe."

"No, Henry. Aven was my mother. Joe is my grandmother. Remember? Joe is at the retirement center with Milford the stalker."

His face relaxed a little. He nodded. "Right."

"How long were you an orphan?" I asked him.

He removed his glasses and rubbed at his eyes. Then with a shaky hand he put them back on. "Hi, honey," he said. "Can I get you something?"

I shook my head and took another bite of my ice cream. "You already did, Henry."

"You seem awfully sad," he said. "Is Joe okay?"

"Joe's fine." I gazed out the windows of the soda shop at the sky, which was turning pink and orange. Sundown syndrome. "She's at the retirement center."

He smiled. "That sounds like a nice place."

"It is, Henry. You've been there."

His eyes lit up. "Have I?"

I nodded. "Yes, you have. A few times."

"Oh. So tell me, little Aven. How many boyfriends do you have right now?" He gave me a wink like he thought he was cheering me up when his words made me feel like garbage.

"Zero," I said. "I have zero boyfriends."

"Zero!" Henry declared. "I bet they're breaking down your door."

I groaned. "Is there, like, a book out there called *Talking to Teenagers for Old People*? Because I swear you all say the same things."

Henry looked around. "Who's old?" he said, then chuckled. "*Aha!*" He pointed at my face. "There's that beautiful smile. That's the one the boys will go wild for."

My smile fell. "No, they won't. No one will ever like me like that."

We don't have to talk.
It's you and me.
We don't have to talk.
We can just be.

—Kids from Alcatraz

ON SUNDAY, I WAS LYING ON THE
couch, watching TV, blissfully alone since Mom had
to drive to some warehouse in Phoenix to pick up an
overdue T-shirt order, trying to think of a good lie to
get out of school the next day, when there was a knock
at the door.

Whoever it was could go away. I didn't care. Then I
heard the bark.

Oh, *shoot*.

I got up and opened the door. "She lives!" Connor
cried out. His smile dissolved. "You look terrible."

"Thanks." I walked back to the couch and sat down.
"I forgot you were coming over today."

"Yeah, it's hard to remind you when you won't answer your phone."

"My battery's been dead."

"Liar. It rang six times every time I called. When it's dead, it doesn't ring at all. It goes straight to voice mail."

I scowled at him. "Who are you, Sherlock Holmes?"

Connor collapsed down on the couch next to me. "So why are your pants on fire, liar, liar?" He glanced at the TV screen. "And why are you watching a show about off-grid living?"

"Research," I told him. "For my life as a hermit."

Connor nodded. "I've tried the hermit life. It's lonely. You wouldn't last a day. You're far too social."

"I'm making some big changes in my life," I said. "Being less social is definitely one of them."

He stared at me. "What's up with you?"

I stared back at him. "What's up with *you*? Why are you so chipper?"

He shrugged, blinked his eyes a few times, barked. "School's just going a lot better than I expected. "

"You mean because of *Amanda*?" I tried to hide my disdain when I said her name but probably not very well. "Did you two get together after school this week like you wanted?"

"Yes." Connor poked me in the ribs. "What's wrong?

Are you jealous?" He teased me. "You shouldn't be. I heard you like someone."

I shot up from the couch. "I do not. Who told you that?"

Connor seemed surprised at my reaction. "Zion. He said you liked this jerk Joshua who used to make fun of him when he was in seventh grade. He—"

"That's not true," I said. "I don't like him at all. When did Zion tell you that?"

"Last weekend. When we were here."

I sat back down on the couch. "I don't like him at all. Zion's right. He's a huge jerk."

Connor stared at me. "Are you okay, Aven? You're not acting like yourself."

"Maybe this is the new me." I stuck my chin out. "Older and wiser. Never to be duped again. Never again the dupee."

"Who duped you?"

I turned back to my show. "No one important."

We sat there quietly side by side, learning all about composting toilets, which are apparently a great choice for off-grid living. I made a mental note.

"Well, this is fun," Connor said. "Don't you want to talk about anything at all?"

"I think I'll try to get one of those composting toilets."

"Can we talk about something that's not toilets?"

I sighed. "How are things going with your dad?"

Connor rolled his eyes. "He keeps trying to do all kinds of 'bonding' activities with me." Connor did air quotes again when he said *bonding*. He laid his head back against the couch and blinked his eyes rapidly. "I know what you're going to say."

"What?"

"That I should do them. That anyone can change. That everyone deserves a second chance." He clucked his tongue.

I stared at the TV. "I wasn't going to say anything like that at all. Not at all."

"Wow, you're really not acting like yourself," Connor mumbled. We sat in silence while the show moved on to the subject of wind turbines. Connor turned his head to me. "Are you planning on getting yourself a wind turbine as well?"

"Sounds like I'll need one."

"This show is maybe the most boring thing I've ever seen. Why don't we play something?"

I relented, and we played video games for a couple of hours. I almost didn't think about my Great Humiliation for a few minutes of that.

Connor's mom knocked on the door as we were

putting the controllers away. "As exciting as this visit has been, I have to go now."

I glowered at the floor. "I'm sorry I haven't been very good company today."

Connor walked toward the door. "That's okay. I'll take a cranky Aven over most other people any day."

"I'm glad you feel that way because I think this is the new me. Or at least the new me for the next four years."

"Then I look forward to four years from now."

"Me too," I grumbled.

Cover my eyes.
Cover my ears.
I don't want to see.
And I don't want to hear.

—We Are Librarians

MOM WOKE ME UP FOR SCHOOL

the next morning. "I'm sick," I told her.

She sat down on my bed. "Aven, I don't know what happened last week, but I wish you would tell me."

I buried my face in my pillow. "Nothing happened. I'm just sick."

I could feel her stare boring into the back of my head like she had superhero laser eyes. "Whatever it was, you can't hide from it, and lie about it, forever. Life goes on."

"Why can't I be homeschooled?" I said into my pillow, my voice all muffled.

"Because I have to work here at the park. And I don't know how to teach you algebra." She tried pushing my hair away from my face, but I buried it deeper into my pillow. "And you can't hide from life."

"Maybe I don't want to *do* life anymore."

"Well, I'm sorry to disappoint you, but you've kind of got to keep doing life until you die a little old lady at the Golden Sunset Retirement Community. Maybe by then they'll have a hot tub and shrimp on the menu."

"I don't want to eat shrimp." I flipped over and faced her. "And I don't want to go to school. I want to stay here in this room. Forever."

Mom cringed. "It's going to smell terrible. You'll stink yourself out."

"No, I won't. I'll still shower."

"How will you shower if you never leave this room?"

"I'll take sponge baths."

She sniffed at the air. "Maybe you should sponge bath it up right now before you go to school."

I sat up, my hair a tangled mess of red around my face. I gave her the crankiest look I was capable of. "You're not going to let this school thing go, are you?"

She shook her head and put an arm around me. "No, I'm not." She squeezed me to her and kissed the top of my head. "Tell you what, though." She tilted my chin up and kissed my nose. "You don't have to ride the toaster oven on wheels today. I'll drive you."

● ● ●

"I am not eating in the cafeteria," I told Zion when I found him sitting on a bench outside waiting for me. "You can't make me!" I borderline yelled at him.

He shrugged. "I'm not fighting you on this. You're going to get burned, though, sitting outside."

"*Aha!*" I cried. "I brought sunblock. So there."

"Well, I guess you've thought of everything."

"I have. I'll see you later," I said, bolting toward my first class of the day.

Zion and I sat under one of the ramadas eating our lunch together. "Thanks for eating outside with me today," I told him. "I know it's hot."

Sweat poured down Zion's forehead and into his eyes. He wiped at them, then took a bite of his banana. "It's not that hot," he said. "I mean, I think I might pass out at any moment. Wake me up if that happens. You do have smelling salts, right?"

"I just can't bear to go in there." I looked around. "*They'll* be in there."

Zion nodded, wiped at his forehead. I knew he was a real friend because he had big ole pit sweat for me. That was some serious loyalty. I should have trusted his judgment about everything else. "They're going to be in there for the next three years," he said. "Is this how it's going to be again?"

I sulked as I chewed a fruit snack. "No."

"Just think—we'd be in there in the nice air conditioning if only you'd listened to me."

I squinted my eyes at Zion, partially from the bright sun, but mostly because I didn't need him to keep telling me that. I knew. I knew I should have listened to him. I was about to tell him as much when Lando walked by with Janessa and some friends. "Why the heck are you guys eating out here in this heat?" Lando said as he threw his backpack onto our table and sat down next to me.

I looked at Zion, and he shrugged. "Change of scenery," he said.

"Dude," Lando said. "You look like you're about to fall over. And those giant sweaty pits are not going to go over well with the ladies." Then he turned me. "How are you feeling, Aven?"

"Why?"

"Because you've been sick," Lando said. "You were sick all week. I was worried about you."

"Why?"

Lando laughed. "Are you always this suspicious?"

"I just don't understand why you'd care."

Lando grabbed his chest. "Ouch. Straight to the heart. So what did you have?"

Oh my gosh. What did I have? I couldn't think of anything. "Botulism," I blurted out. "I had botulism."

Lando looked from me to Zion. Zion nodded seriously. "Yes, that's what she had."

"Geez," Lando said. "We learned about that in bio."

Oh, *shoot.*

"That's really serious," Lando went on. "And rare. Like super rare. You're lucky to be alive. How'd you get it?"

I shook my head. Lying was a dangerous game, all right. "Oh, did I say botulism? I meant I had... bronchitis."

Lando seemed confused. "I guess . . . I can see how you'd make that mistake." He laughed. "They both start with *b*. But you sound like you're breathing pretty well now."

I took a deep breath. "Bronchioles all clear," I declared.

Lando smiled. "Have you found a costume for Comic Con yet?"

I shook my head. "I don't think I'm going to go."

"What?" Zion and Lando cried out at the same time.

"You have to go," Lando said. "It's going to be so much fun."

"I don't know," I said. "I'm kind of aiming for this hermit lifestyle, and stuff like Comic Con doesn't fit into that."

Lando slapped his hand down on the table. "You could go as Hermit!"

I laughed—the first time in a week. "There's a comic book character named Hermit?"

"Yeah," Lando said. "There's pretty much every kind of comic book character you can think of, so you have your pick. Also, I've been trying to get Zion to go to homecoming. Why don't the two of you go together?"

Zion and I both scrunched up our noses at each other.

"I mean as friends, of course," Lando said. "Geez, you guys."

"Zion wouldn't want to go with me anyway," I said. "I think there's someone else he'd rather go with."

"Who?" Lando asked.

Zion kicked my leg. "Aven!"

"Why don't you just ask her?" I said. "She *is* home-schooled. She told me she wished she could go to school dances. And she thinks you're cute." I totally made up that last part, but I hoped it was true. *Sheesh.* Lying was getting easier and easier with every passing minute.

Zion's eyes widened. "Did she say that?"

Lando threw up his hands. "Oh my gosh. Please tell me who you're talking about."

"Trilby," I said.

"Aven!" Zion cried again.

"Ask her," I said. "Or how about this? I'll talk to her about it and see how she feels."

Zion played with his banana peel on the picnic table. "If I agree to let you talk to her, you have to do something, too."

"What?"

"You have to go with us."

Lando nodded. "Yep. That sounds like a fair deal."

Just a week ago, I would have been excited at the idea. Definitely not anymore. Why would I set myself up like that to get humiliated again? "No way am I going to any dance. You do know what happens at school dances, don't you?"

Zion's mouth dropped open. "Yeah, Aven, I do. People dance. It's a nightmare."

"They don't just dance," I said. I leaned in and whispered. "They do the 'Y.M.C.A.'"

Zion scrunched up his face. "Why does that mat—" Understanding flooded his face. "*Ohhhhhhh.*"

"Yeah," I said. "Exactly."

"You could always do it with your feet," Lando said. "We'll do it with you."

"Yeah, that's nice of you to offer, but I think I'll pass."

"You have to go," Lando went on. "If Zion and Trilby go—"

"Big if!" Zion cried

Lando punched his brother on the arm. "We'll still have an extra seat in the van. It needs a butt in it."

"Or what?" I asked.

Lando smiled. "Or we'll be one butt short."

Zion shrugged. "You agree to go or I don't ask Trilby."

"It's me who'd be asking her," I said. Man, I wanted so badly to see Zion go to the dance with Trilby. I couldn't be the one to hold him back. I sat there a moment imagining the whole scene: Trilby showing up looking amazingly cute with some new bright streaks in her hair—maybe orange. She and Zion dancing. Maybe she'd let Zion kiss her on the cheek. The incredible progress that could be made with Zion's confidence was earth shattering.

Zion stared at me, his eyes squinted to slits.

"Fine," I said. "I'll ask her if she'd like to go with *both of us*."

And just as I was starting to feel the slightest bit better, the absolute worst thing that could have happened happened: Joshua walked by. "Hey, Aven," he called and blew me a kiss.

I whipped away from him.

Don't cry don't cry don't cry.

Lando watched Joshua as he walked into the cafeteria. Then he turned to us. "What was that all about?"

Zion took a big bite of his banana. "I don't know," he said, his mouth full.

Lando looked at me. I shrugged. "I don't know."

Don't cry don't cry don't cry.

Zion swallowed his bite of banana. "Oh, yeah. He told me I should go to Comic Con as Blob."

Lando clenched his jaw. "I can't stand that guy. I can't believe he's still saying stuff like that to you. I'd kick his butt if it wouldn't get me thrown off the football team."

Don't cry don't cry don't cry.

"It sucks so bad we have to be on the same team together. He's such a jerk."

Don't cry don't cry don't cry.

16

Don't you ever tire
Of being a liar
And your pants being on fire?

—Screaming Ferret

I WALKED INTO THE GOLDEN SUNSET

Retirement Community after school that day. Josephine was in the leisure room as usual, reading some terrible book. As usual. This week's selection had a pirate with a hairy chest on the cover.

I sat down next to her on the couch. "You should be embarrassed to read those books in public," I said.

She set it down on the table next to her. "Why should I be? They have them all here in the library. Obviously they intend for someone to read them."

"Don't they have any, like, quality reading material here?"

"This is quality," Josephine insisted. "Listen to this

writing." She licked her finger then turned back a few pages.

"Oh, gosh, please don't read that out loud." I glanced around at all the old people. "Someone's going to have a stroke if you read that out loud."

Josephine ignored me and read: "'Demetrius's love for Antonia was as vast as the universe, as endless as the sea, as deep as the deepest pit on earth. It was an unstoppable force, a ship slicing through the choppiest of waters.'"

I snorted. "That's the cheesiest thing I've ever heard."

"'Demetrius would wait until the end of time for Antonia—'"

"Oh my gosh, and you're still reading."

"'He would wait until he was nothing more than a skeleton, his bones unearthed by an archeologist hundreds of years from now.'" She narrowed her eyes at me. "'*Pirate bones.*'"

I couldn't keep from laughing. "That is the worst writing I've ever heard."

Josephine slammed the book shut and threw it down on the coffee table. "Aren't we the snooty connoisseur of fine literature?" she said in a huff.

I smiled at her. "I'm sorry I've hurt your feelings.

You know, I think I feel better after you read that to me. I needed a good laugh."

She sulked on the couch next to me as Milford shuffled up to us. I looked down and saw he had thankfully exchanged his Bert and Ernie slippers for some blue sneakers.

"Hi, Josephine," he said, his cheeks pink.

"Hello, Milford," Josephine said without making eye contact with him. "What can I do for you?"

"Oh, nothing," Milford said. "I just wanted to tell you how nice your hair looks today."

Josephine shot him an evil look. "Are you serious? I always look my worst on Mondays."

"Why?" I asked her.

"Because I have my hair done on Tuesdays, of course!"

I had to admit—one side of her head was awfully flat. But Milford smiled at her. "Well, I think you look lovely," he said. "Like a new blossom on a beautiful spring day."

Josephine groaned, but I said, "Hey, that sounds like a line out of one of your books."

Milford beamed with pride as Josephine glared at him. "Why don't you go eat some chess pieces?" she said.

His smile fell, and he ambled over to the chessboard.

I turned to Josephine. "You are so mean to him."

"I want him to leave me alone."

"But he likes you."

Josephine *humphed*. "No, he don't."

"Yes, he clearly does."

"He does not," Josephine insisted. "Men like that are only after one thing."

I looked at Milford, sitting over the chessboard, shoulders slumped. "I know. You already said that, but I still don't understand what that is."

"Someone to clean up after them."

"But you have housekeeping here."

"Someone to cook them all their meals."

"But you all eat in the cafeteria. No one cooks here."

"Someone to keep track of all their medicine."

"But you have nurses to do that for you."

Josephine jerked her head at me. "Well, don't you have an answer for everything?" She picked her book up and thumbed through the pages.

"Can I ask you something?"

"What?" she grumbled, her face hidden behind her book.

"Do you know if Henry has any family?"

She peeked over the top of her book at me. "Henry? No, Henry's never had any family. Why you asking?"

"It's just that he's so old. Like really, really old. Even older than you."

Josephine grunted and lifted her book so I couldn't see her face again.

"If something happened to him, who would we call?"

"You'd call me," she said. "The almost really, really old person."

"But you're not his family."

"Well, I'm the closest he's got."

"He told me he was an orphan, like, in an actual orphanage."

"Yep."

"Do you know anything else about it?"

"Nope."

"Don't you care about whether he has family or not?"

"Like I said, Henry ain't got no family."

I laid my head back against the couch. "Fine," I said through clenched teeth. We sat there awhile in silence as I watched the other people in the room. One woman hobbled by us pushing a walker, and I found myself suddenly terrified of getting old. How would I push a walker? What would I do when I lost the flexibility in my legs?

"So tell me what's going on with school," Josephine

said, tearing me away from my alarming thoughts. "Everything going all right?"

I let out another long, loud breath as I stared up at the paneled ceiling.

"That good, huh?"

"I'm considering homeschooling right now."

"And what does your mother have to say about that?"

I sat up straight. "She's completely against it," I said with total indignation.

"Uh-huh."

"There's always online school."

"Uh-huh."

"And if I'm going to be a hermit, I don't need a lot of education anyway. I just need to know how to operate composting toilets and wind turbines and solar panels and stuff like that. We don't even have farming as an elective at my school."

"A hermit, huh? That sounds awfully lonely."

"It sounds awfully awesome."

"I don't think it sounds awesome at all." Josephine flipped a page. "Nope. Not at all."

I clenched my teeth. "Everyone is being so unsupportive of my life plans."

"That's because your life plans stink right now."

I glared at Josephine. "Maybe I should track down my bio father so I can try to get someone on my side."

"Good luck finding him."

"How *would* I find him? You know something about him, don't you?"

"I already told you I don't know nothin' about that man."

"Yeah, like you don't know nothin' about Henry's family. Boy, you just don't know nothin' about nothin'."

She glared at me over her book. "I know lots about important stuff."

"Yeah, like pirate bones. Aven never told you *anything* about him? Anything at all?"

Josephine stared at her book. "I told you all I know.

"But you two were so close."

Josephine pursed her lips. "You think I'm lying to you?"

"Well, you've lied about other things."

"Like what?"

"The fact that you're my grandmother."

"I most certainly did not lie about that." She flipped a page. "I withheld information."

"Same thing."

"No, it's not. When you asked me, I told you."

"Are you withholding information now?"

"Why the sudden interest in your father anyway?

The guy is probably a bum." She motioned at Milford with her head. "Like Milford over there."

"Milford is not a bum."

Josephine rolled her eyes. "What about that boy who likes you?"

My stomach clenched, and I felt like I might barf all over Josephine's cheesy pirate book. "What boy?"

"That boy you told me about at school. Anything happening with him?"

"No. He doesn't like me. Forget about it."

She put her book down. "What happened?"

"Nothing happened. He just doesn't like me."

"How do you know that?"

I *so* did not want to talk about this anymore. "I just know. He's a jerk. A big, fat, huge, enormous jerk."

"What did he do to you?"

"Nothing."

"Now who's the one withholding information?"

I looked away from Josephine. "I don't know. Who?"

Josephine *humphed* and lifted her book up in front of her face again. "How's horse-riding lessons going?"

I grimaced. "Isn't there anything we can talk about that doesn't make me want to barf?"

"We could talk about my book."

"Try again."

Being punk
Isn't about clothes and junk.
It's about freeing your mind
From social confines.

—The Square Pegs

I SAT ON CHILI. WHY DID IT ALWAYS have to be so hot when I had my lessons? Maybe because it was hot every day. Every. Stinking. Day.

"Don't worry," my dad would tell me in the evening. "It's about to start cooling down soon." But cool weather was starting to feel like nothing but a distant memory.

"Let's practice moving Chili up a gait today," Bill said as he placed my helmet on my head and snapped it. "We don't need to worry about the jump if you don't feel ready."

I nodded then turned to Chili. "Down," I ordered her. She lowered to the ground, and I swung a leg over the top of her. I pressed my feet into the stirrups. "Stand."

Chili stood, and Bill patted her nose. "You're such a smart horse. Aren't you, girl?"

I tapped her sides gently with my feet and said, "Walk." We moved around the arena for a couple of laps like that until I got up the nerve to cluck my tongue at her, moving her into a trot. I always felt like I was going to flop right out of the saddle when we started trotting, but I concentrated on staying as steady as possible.

"Move her up to a canter," Bill called to me from across the arena. Even though we'd cantered just a couple of weeks ago, my stomach knotted up at the thought of going any faster.

I shook my head. "I don't want to," I cried. "I'll fall off."

"You won't fall off," Bill yelled back. "You've gotten strong."

"I'm not strong," I cried. And I knew when I said it that it was true. I wasn't strong enough to ride a horse. I wasn't strong enough to stand up for myself. I wasn't strong enough to face high school.

"Whoa," I told Chili as I pulled back on the stirrups with my legs. The reins attached to them pulled on Chili's head and she stopped. We stood there for a moment in the heat, both of us breathing heavily.

Bill ran over. "Why'd you stop? You were doing so well."

"I don't want to canter today."

"But you were doing so well with it just a couple of weeks ago. What's happened?"

"I'm just . . . not ready for all this."

Bill patted Chili's nose again. "You *are* ready. You seem to have lost your confidence. You just need to find it again."

Well, if that was all I needed then I was really in trouble.

"Let's practice turning some more," Bill said.

So I turned Chili—left, right, left, right—until the lesson ended.

"You're making good progress," Bill said as he pulled the saddle off Chili. Every time he did that, I thought how wonderful it must have felt for her to get that hot, sweaty thing off—like the same way I felt when my helmet came off. "I don't want you to stress out about it."

I stared at the floor of the stall. But I *was* stressed out about it. I was stressed out about everything. And Bill was just being nice—I wasn't making good progress at all. I was going backward.

I sat down on a small stool in the stall and Bill helped me remove one of my boots. Then he handed me a brush. I took it with my foot. "I think you should spend some quality time in here with her." He picked up the saddle. "I'm going to go put this away and clean up the tack room. You two need some good bonding time."

I sat on the stool and stared at Chili, only the two of us now in the stall. "Did you hear that?" I said. "Bill wants us to bond." I got up and stood in front of her. I stared into her deep brown eyes. She nosed my face and licked at my red hair. Then she put her head down to my bare foot.

I smiled. "You really are a smart girl," I said as I rubbed at her head with my toes. Then I picked up the brush with my foot and did my best to brush her sides while sitting on the stool. I could only go so high, but I knew Bill would do a better job later.

Bill came back into the stall and placed a bucket with some carrots in it next to me. "She'll love these," he said. "They're nice and cold—right out of the fridge."

I fed Chili one carrot at a time with my foot while Bill finished brushing her down, then I made my way to see Trilby. I still had to talk to her about homecoming.

I kicked a little at the door of Sonoran Smoothies. She glanced up and gave me a funny look. I kicked again. *Why don't you come in?* she mouthed.

I shook my head. I didn't want to smell the smoothies in there. I once read that our smell memory is our strongest memory. If I set foot in Sonoran Smoothies and smelled the smoothies, it would be like reliving my Great Humiliation, not that I wasn't already reliving it fifty times a day. But I guess that was still better than fifty-one times a day.

Trilby came outside. "What are you doing out here, Aven?"

"I can't come in," I said. "But I wanted to talk to you about something."

"What?"

"You know how you said that one thing you didn't like about being homeschooled was that you wouldn't get to go to any school dances?"

"Yeah?"

"Well, Zion and I want to go to the homecoming dance for our school, you know, as friends. I mean, Zion's not my boyfriend or anything like that, and I know they're going to play that manufactured music you don't like, but we were hoping you'd come with us. Come with him. Come with us."

I wasn't sure what to expect from Trilby, but I was happy when her face lit up. "Really?" She jumped up and threw her arms around me. "That would be so much fun."

I was filled with both a mixture of happiness for Zion that Trilby would be going to homecoming with us and annoyance for myself that I now had to go as well. But I liked to think that my happiness for Zion outweighed my annoyance for myself. Or at least that it was evenly split—fifty-fifty. At worst—forty-sixty.

I peeked in on Henry and saw he was busy taking care of customers. He seemed like he was having a good day, so I made my way home to take a cool shower. Then I sat down at our kitchen table with my parents. No matter how busy we all were, how hectic things were at the park, we always tried to sit down every night for dinner together.

"So I've decided to go to the homecoming dance," I told them.

Mom dropped her chicken leg onto the table and threw her hands over her mouth.

"Oh my gosh," I pleaded. "Please don't overreact. It's just a dance."

"My baby's first dance," she said, her voice muffled through her hands. "We'll have to get you a new dress."

"Yeah," Dad agreed. He waggled his eyebrows at me. "I hear pink ribbons and ruffles are all the rage in high school these days."

"Definitely not," I told Dad. "And they also don't say stuff like *all the rage*, either."

Dad grinned. "Then I hear they're *hip*."

Mom casually picked at her chicken leg. "So is a boy going with you?"

"Just Zion. And Trilby is going with us, too."

"Trilby from the smoothie shop?" Dad asked.

I nodded. "Yeah, she's cool." I glared at Mom. "Probably because she's homeschooled."

"Now if you were homeschooled you wouldn't be going to homecoming, would you?"

"Trilby's homeschooled, and she's going to homecoming."

Mom brushed my comment away with a wave of her hand.

"Trilby listens to punk rock, you know," I said. "Her dad was even in a punk band."

"Robert?" Dad said. "But he seems so *normal*."

"I didn't realize you had to be abnormal to be in a punk band."

Dad scrunched up his nose. "No, I just meant he seems so, you know . . . *normal*."

Mom rolled her eyes. "Really, Ben, you are so uncool."

"I am not uncool," Dad said. "I just thought punk band people had a lot of tattoos and piercings and wore ripped clothing. Maybe a Mohawk. Robert's hair is completely normal." He raised his eyebrows. "And I've seen him wear a *polo shirt* before."

"Punk is about what you are on the inside, not what you look like on the outside," I said.

"Oh, I like that," Mom said. "I think I should check out some punk music."

"I'll play some for you. I've found a bunch of good bands."

"Cool." Mom clasped her hands together excitedly in front of her face. "We'll bond over punk music."

Dad gave Mom an incredulous look. "I can't see you enjoying punk rock, Laura."

Mom dropped her hands on the table and glared at him. "You don't know what you're talking about."

He snorted. "You have Taylor Swift on your Favorites playlist."

"What's wrong with Taylor Swift?" Mom cried.

"Nothing. Just pretty sure she's not very punk rock," Dad said.

I decided to change the subject before things got seriously heated, and Dad mentioned that Mom also had Justin Bieber on there. "You know, I think Josephine might know something about my father she's not telling me."

"Your bio father?" Mom asked.

I picked up my chicken wing with my toes and took a bite. "Yeah, she's awfully evasive about it when I ask her."

Dad stared at me. "Have you been asking her about him a lot?"

I shrugged. "A little, I guess."

"What is it you want to know, honey?" Mom asked.

"Anything," I said. "I don't know anything at all about him."

"And Josephine can't tell you anything?" Dad asked, looking down at his plate, pushing his chicken thigh around.

"She says she can't, but I'm not sure she's being completely truthful. She gets all shifty-eyed when I ask her about him."

"Shifty-eyed, huh?" said Mom.

I dropped my chicken wing from my toes onto my plate and sat up straight. "Yeah, like this." I made my eyes dart back and forth around the room.

"Well, I don't know why she'd lie to you," Mom said. "If she says she doesn't know anything, then I'm sure she doesn't."

"Maybe she's trying to protect me," I said.

"From what?" Dad asked.

"Maybe my father is someone awful."

"Not a chance," Mom said. "No one awful made my baby."

"Maybe he's something truly terrible. Like an animal euthanizer or something."

"I don't think that's an actual job," Dad said.

I narrowed my eyes at them. "Maybe he's a politician."

Mom grimaced. "That would be quite shocking, but I doubt he's a politician. Maybe he's something cool." She smiled. "Maybe *he's* in a punk band."

"Now that would be cool," I said.

"Why all this sudden interest in your father?" Mom asked.

"Just curious."

"Well, you know what they say about curiosity," Mom said.

"It killed the cat."

"Nope," Mom said. "It's the sign of a powerful brain."

I smiled. "Who says that?"

"Science."

It doesn't mean I don't care.
If you only knew.
It's because I care so much
That I get mad at you.

—Kids from Alcatraz

"I HAVE EXCITING NEWS," I TOLD
Zion as I dropped my bag onto the lunch table.

His eyes widened. "What?"

"Trilby wants to go to homecoming with us."

Zion shook his head. "No way. Really? No way."

"Yes way." I pulled my head out from under the shoulder strap. "Which means we're all going together." I sat down. *"Yippee."* I glanced around the lunchroom for a moment.

"Ignore them," Zion said. "Don't even look at their table."

I focused on Zion like I was booby trapped, and if I took my eyes off him for only a moment, I would explode—just a big poof of red hair and gone. "I won't. I'm not. Are they looking at me?"

"No."

"Are you lying?"

"No."

"Do I need to check to see if they're looking at me?"

"No."

I tore my eyes off Zion and stood up to dig through my bag with my feet, searching for my lunch. "Are they watching me?"

"No, Aven. You have to forget about them."

I let out a huge breath. "I will."

"They're not worth it."

"I know." I gave up finding my lunch for a moment and sagged down in my seat.

Zion scowled. "How did your last lesson go?" I could tell he was trying to take my mind off Joshua and his friends.

I gazed at a nearby window. "*Meh.*"

"Did you do the jump yet?"

"*Meh.*"

"Why haven't you done it?"

I moved my eyes from the bright window to Zion. "I can't hold on. I'll fall off." I rolled my eyes. "*Duh.*"

Zion crossed his arms. "*Duh?*"

"Would you want to ride a big roller coaster without a harness?"

"That's not a very good comparison."

"Would you skydive without a parachute?"

"That's worse," Zion said. "Not even close. Just do the jump. Stop being a scaredy-cat."

"No one says *scaredy-cat*."

"I totally just did."

I huffed as I stood back up and started rummaging around in my bag again with my foot. I finally found my protein bar buried at the bottom, all smashed and broken up, and sat down with it. I tore the package open with my toes, but it ripped open too quickly and the little broken pieces went flying all over the table. I let out a huge exasperated sigh.

I stared down at the little crumbly pieces of protein bar scattered all over the table and floor. "I can't go on like this."

"I'll buy you a lunch," Zion said.

"That's not what I meant. I don't think I can do high school."

"You can do it. But listening to me would definitely make your life a lot easier."

"Oh my gosh, I get it!" I cried. "I should have listened to you."

Zion crossed his arms. "*Mm-hm*."

"You know what would definitely make my life a lot easier? If my mom would homeschool me. Then my life would be just fine and dandy."

Zion uncrossed his arms and raised a hand. "*Whoa.* Hold up. You asked your mom to homeschool you?"

I nodded.

"And you didn't check with me first?"

"Check with you about what?"

"If I was okay with that!" Zion shrieked. "You were going to make this decision without my input! Not that I should be surprised. It's not like you care about *anything* I have to say."

I shrunk down in my seat. "Sorry."

"I can't believe you would abandon me to face high school by myself."

"I guess I didn't think "

"No, you didn't." Zion stuffed his lunch back in his backpack and stood up from his seat. "All you're thinking about is yourself." He stormed away from the table.

"Hey!" I called after him, but he ignored me as he left the cafeteria.

He was right, of course. All I'd been thinking about since starting stupid high school was myself. Mostly bad stuff, too. And I had no idea how to stop doing that.

• • •

I walked up the bleacher steps after school and found Zion sitting alone, watching Lando's practice. I sat next to my friend. "I'm sorry."

Zion didn't look at me.

"I should have listened to you about Joshua. Trust me—I know this with all my heart. Please stop being angry with me about it."

He finally moved his eyes to me. "I'm not—"

"Yes, you are. And I totally get it. I didn't consider your feelings then, and I didn't consider your feelings about the homeschooling thing. I didn't think about what that would mean for you. You were right. I've only been thinking about myself. But I'm not going to abandon you. We're going to get through this together."

Zion's face finally softened and his lip turned up a little at one corner.

"We will," I said. "We're going to slay the sucktastic beast known as high school together."

Zion nodded. "Okay."

I peered down in time to see Lando give Joshua a dirty look as he walked by him on the field. "It sucks we can't watch Lando without watching Joshua," I said.

"Tell me about it."

"That guy is the worst."

"The worst in the world," Zion said. "He's so not worth our time."

"He's not even worth our loogies."

Zion and I smiled at each other. "I still need to find a costume for Comic Con," I said. "And I have so little time."

"You don't have to wear one."

"I don't want to be the only one not wearing one. I'll come up with something."

"I'm sure it will be great."

I watched as Joshua walked up to Lando and said something to him. I wished I could hear what they were saying. Lando dropped his water bottle and stepped up into Joshua's face, saying something back. He did not look happy. The coach blew his whistle and stormed over to the two.

Zion jumped up. "Shoot."

I stood up next to him. "What do you think is happening?"

"I don't know."

We couldn't ask Lando what had happened in the car on the way home because we didn't want to rat him out to their mom. So Zion and I sat quietly in the back until we got to their house.

I loved Zion's house. Instead of boring art prints, the

walls were covered in cool framed movie posters and puzzles the family had done together. The phone played "The Imperial March" when it rang, and the lamps turned on and off when you clapped. Trust me, clapping my feet is far easier than turning those annoying little knobs.

Zion and I went to his room so we could work on guitar lessons. His mom had bought him a guitar for his birthday, and he was making great progress.

I pointed my toe at a fret. "Here," I said. "Your finger goes here." We were working on learning songs that stuck to a few basic chords. Today we were doing "Free Fallin'" by Tom Petty, which was made like a million years ago, but it was easy to play.

Zion strummed out a few chords. "Nice," I said. "Now move your finger here." I pointed at another fret.

Zion's mom opened the door and peeked her head in. "Zion, baby? I need your head. I'm not sure the size of this mask is right."

Zion groaned and got up to go get his head fitted. I moved the guitar down to my feet. I strummed out the chords I was teaching Zion and sang the lyrics softly to myself. I wished learning to navigate high school were as easy as learning new songs on the guitar. I wished there were instructions and maybe a YouTube video to tell me exactly what I needed to do.

There was movement in the doorway. I stopped playing and looked up in time to see Lando move away.

My cheeks heated. I still didn't like playing in front of anyone despite having played at the festival, and I definitely didn't like singing in front of anyone. I was embarrassed that he'd seen me.

Zion returned and sat back down on the bed. He picked the guitar up and held it on his lap. "What's this mask?" I asked him.

"She's making a special Batman mask for me."

"That's cool. Don't you already have a Batman mask?"

"Yeah, but this one's going to be *custom*."

I glanced at the open doorway. "What's Lando doing?"

Zion shrugged. "I don't know. Probably talking to his friends as usual."

Zion and I practiced the guitar until his mom told us it was time for "dinner." Another time I wished I had the ability to do air quotes was when I referred to the food we ate at Zion's house as "dinner." The reason why I call it "dinner" is because Zion's family frequently ate appetizers and snacks, which was awesome. I loved eating at Zion's house.

I sat down at the table. Tonight's selections included a tray of deviled eggs, carrots and dip, a bowl of popcorn, cantaloupe slices, and a bowl of mixed nuts.

"Hors d'oeuvres again?" Zion complained as he sat down next to me.

"You know I have to finish my Death Star cross stitch," Mrs. Hill said. "I didn't have time."

Lando smiled. "You never have time to cook, Ma."

"That's because I have so many better things to do. I don't see any of you boys in here whipping up a pot roast." She eyed each of them one by one, ending on Mr. Hill.

Mr. Hill cleared his throat. "How was practice?" He asked Lando as he popped an almond into his mouth. Mr. Hill always wore T-shirts with cool black comic book characters on them. He said they needed all the promotion they could get. Today his T-shirt had Black Lightning on it.

Lando shrugged. "It was all right. Still hotter than biscuits outside."

I snorted. "Straight out of the oven," I grumbled, and Lando smiled as he rammed a handful of popcorn in his mouth.

Mr. Hill turned his attention to me. "Have you picked a costume yet for this weekend, Aven?" I was learning that Mr. Hill took this whole costume business really seriously.

I scowled at the deviled egg filling all over my toes. I should have stuck to the carrots. "Not yet."

"Not yet!" Mr. Hill cried. I could see I was stressing him out.

"Dad," Zion pleaded.

"What are you going as, Mr. Hill?" I asked, trying to take the focus off me.

He pointed as his Black Lightning T-shirt and smiled. "What do you think?"

"Cool," I said.

Mrs. Hill had a mischievous smile as she munched on some cantaloupe. "Mine is a surprise."

"I can't wait." I looked at Lando. "What are you going as?"

"Mine's a surprise, too," he said.

"So many secrets in this family," I said.

"We like surprises," said Mrs. Hill. "Don't you like to be surprised, Aven?"

"I don't think so."

As Zion helped his parents clear the table, I asked Lando, "Were you spying on me earlier?"

Lando gulped down his bite of carrot. "Spying on you?"

"Earlier. When I was playing the guitar."

"Oh. No, I wasn't spying. I heard the guitar and I thought it was Zion. I thought he'd somehow gotten not completely terrible."

Zion ran over and wrapped his arms around Lando's head from behind like he was choking him. Lando fell backward out of his chair, and then they were trying to pin each other down on the ground.

"Someone's gonna get hurt," Mrs. Hill said, but she didn't seem too terribly worried as she loaded the dishwasher.

I laughed as Lando smashed a deviled egg into Zion's ear and Zion screamed. Zion got up and poured the rest of the popcorn bowl on Lando's head.

"What a mess," Mrs. Hill muttered, but I suddenly wished I had a sibling whose ear I could smash a deviled egg into.

Mom picked me up after Lando and Zion had sufficiently destroyed each other and the kitchen with their battle.

I gazed out the car window at the passing streetlights as we drove the short distance from Zion's house to Stagecoach Pass. "Sometimes I wish I had a brother or sister," I said.

I turned to Mom, but she stared straight ahead. "Oh, yeah?" she said softly.

"Yeah. I mean, I'm good with being an only child. Just sometimes I think it would be nice to have one." I turned back to the window. "That's all."

Mom was quiet, so I kept talking. "I wonder if my birth father ever had any other children."

Mom squeezed the steering wheel. "I don't know. I suppose it's certainly possible."

"I could have brothers and sisters I don't even know about."

Mom nodded slowly. She cleared her throat. "Would you want to try to find that out?"

I shrugged and looked back out the dark window. "I don't know. I wouldn't know where to start." Mom didn't respond to that, and she was quiet the rest of the way home, so I didn't mention it again.

I sat down at my computer as soon as we got home. No more messing around. I was going to figure out my costume. I remembered Lando saying there was just about any comic book character you could think of.

I stuck my ear buds in and turned on some Llama Parade while I browsed for ideas online. On a whim, I Googled "Armless comic book characters" and . . .

Oh. My. Gosh.

*You didn't have a clue
You were a fascist,
Did you?*

—Screaming Ferret

MOM FRANTICALLY HELPED ME

gather all the materials I needed to make my costume, which basically amounted to a bunch of yellow spandex and a pair of black spandex shorts. I was ready to show up at Zion's house in all of my amazing costume glory just in time for Comic Con. I couldn't wait to see the looks on everyone faces when they saw the character I'd chosen. He seemed pretty obscure, so I wondered if they'd know him.

Mom dropped me off at Zion's, and I kicked gently on the door. Mrs. Hill answered with a big toothy smile, all dressed in green spandex (seriously, what was up with comic book characters and spandex?) and a long flowing black wig.

"She-Hulk!" I cried.

She flexed her foam muscles for me, then she took in my costume. Her smile faded.

I looked down at all my spandex, worried one of my butt cheeks was somehow exposed. "What?" I asked her.

"Nothing."

"Do you know who I am?"

Her frown deepened. "I think so."

"Well, what's wrong?" I said, following her into the living room. "Isn't it amazing?"

All she said was, "*Uhhhhhh.*"

Zion walked into the room wearing his custom Batman mask and cape. He pulled his mask off. "What the heck are you supposed to be?" he said to me.

I jumped into the middle of the living room with great flourish and announced, "I am Armless Tiger Man!"

"Oh," Zion said, not nearly as impressed as I'd hoped. "I totally forgot he existed."

Lando ran into the room. He stepped up onto the coffee table and did a full foamy muscle bodybuilding show for us, doing every pose and flex imaginable. I laughed. "Captain America," I said.

"You guessed it." Lando jumped down from the coffee table.

"It was a tough one," I said. "With all the red, white, and blue and the big ole *A* on your forehead."

"But I'm not just Captain America. I'm Isaiah Bradley." Lando stopped his flexing long enough to scan me up and down. "And you are . . . " His hands shot to his mouth. "Oh my gosh." He laughed under his hands.

"What? What's the big deal?" I jumped up on the coffee table as Lando had, but not nearly as gracefully, and announced, "I am Armless Tiger Man and proud of it!"

Lando laughed harder. "That is *so* not something to be proud of, Aven."

"You should have told me your plans," Zion said to me. "I could have explained it to you."

"Explained what to me? I wanted it to be a surprise. Remember? This family loves their surprises."

"Yeah, *good* surprises," Zion said.

"What's not good about my surprise?"

Lando was laughing so hard he could barely speak anymore. Zion's face was serious, though. "You don't know anything about Armless Tiger Man, do you?"

"I know he doesn't have arms, which means he's awesome. And that he's a *super-villain* which makes him even awesomer." I looked around the room at everyone, but they seemed unconvinced. "His ability to use his feet like hands is listed as a superpower." I stood there and waited for this information to sink in. Didn't they realize what it meant? "I have an actual *real* super-power," I whispered.

"Honey, I love that you have a real superpower," Mrs. Hill said. "But how did you even find out about Armless Tiger Man?"

I shrugged. "I Googled 'Armless comic book characters.' I couldn't believe there actually was one. Pretty lucky."

Zion's mom shook her head. "Oh, honey, no. No, not lucky."

"You must not have read much more about him than that he doesn't have arms," Lando said between laughing gasps.

"Well, I didn't exactly have a lot of time."

There was a knock on the door, and Mrs. Hill opened it. Connor walked in wearing a dog costume. "What are you?" I asked him.

He barked. "Guess."

"Krypto," said Mrs. Hill.

"Nope," said Connor.

"Lockjaw," said Mrs. Hill.

"Nope."

"Wonder Dog."

"Nope."

"Cosmo the Space Dog."

"Nope."

"Dylan Dog."

"Nope."

"Geez," I said. "How many dog comic book characters are there?"

"A lot," said Mrs. Hill, then she jumped up and down. "*Oh, oh, oh*! Lucky the Pizza Dog!"

"Yes!" said Connor. "I can bark all day long and no one will think anything of it. Comic Con is going to be amazing." He looked me up and down. "What are you exactly?"

I shrugged. "Everyone's apparently all horrified that I came as Armless Tiger Man for some reason."

Connor's eyes widened. "That's a real thing?"

"Yeah, can you believe it?" I said.

"Come here," Lando said, leading me into a room with floor to ceiling bookshelves filled with comic books on every wall.

"Whoa, this is so cool." I scanned over the shelves while Lando flipped through a book on a small desk. "What's that?"

Lando took off his Captain America Mask and set it down. "My parents have all the comic books catalogued here so they're easy to find."

I stopped in front of a glass case. "What are these?"

"Those are the most valuable ones. One in there is worth ten thousand dollars."

"Seriously?"

"Here it is," Lando said. He thumbed over a row of comic books then pulled one out. He flipped through it a moment, then placed it open on the floor in front of me. "Read this."

I sat down and read, turning the page with a toe. My mouth dropped open. "*Ew*. Armless Tiger Man is a cannibal?"

Lando snickered. "That's not all."

I flipped another page. "Oh my gosh! And a Nazi!" I flipped more pages. "I'm a cannibalistic Nazi!" I shrieked.

Lando was laughing so hard he was bent over, holding his stomach. He finally came up for air to tell me, "You should have been more thorough in your research."

I fell back on the carpet, the comic book still under my foot. "I'm like the worst comic book character ever."

"No, I'm sure there are worse ones," Lando said.

I stared up at the ceiling. "Like who?"

"The Red Bee has a trained bumblebee."

"A trained bumblebee would be amazing."

"Almighty Dollar is an accountant who shoots pennies from his hands."

"I wish I could do that. I'm broke all the time."

"Bouncing Boy blows up and bounces around like a human bouncy ball."

"That would be so much fun."

"One of Walrus's superpowers is being good at crossword puzzles."

"I'd love that. I'm terrible at crossword puzzles."

"Asbestos Lady wears a suit made of actual asbestos."

"Why?"

"Because it's fireproof."

"Yeah, that one's pretty bad, but it's still not as bad as Armless Tiger Man."

"Dogwelder welds dogs to people's faces."

I laughed and sat up. "You're making that one up."

Lando shook his head. "Nope. I can find him for you." He searched through the reference book again and brought me a comic, setting it down in front of me. We both giggled as we read about Dogwelder together.

"Oh, there's also Eye Scream," Lando said.

"Ice cream?"

"No. Eye. Scream."

"Oh, man. Does he scream with his eyes?"

"No, he can turn himself into any flavor ice cream he wants."

"Then why isn't he called Ice Cream? I don't get it."

"Yeah, it's bizarre."

"He's still a way better character than Armless Tiger Man, though. I would immediately turn myself into mint chip. And then I would eat myself for being so stupid and dressing like Armless Tiger Man."

We sat on the floor together a moment. I looked up and found Lando staring at me, not really smiling. I moved my eyes back to the comic book. "I can't believe there are all these comic book characters. Who comes up with this stuff?"

Lando closed the comic book with Dogwelder in it and returned it to its proper place on the shelf. "Lots of writers and artists."

"How do you know about them?"

Lando waved his arms around. "Did you notice the room you're in?"

"Have you read all of these?"

"No, but a ton of them. I'm sort of fascinated with all the different characters. Like, what are people thinking when they write this weird stuff? And I love the art."

"Maybe you should write a comic book," I said.

Lando smiled. "I am already."

"Really? Can I read it?"

He shrugged and put his Captain America mask back on. "Maybe. One day. It's not ready."

I stood up. "Okay."

"Oh, I forgot to tell you one more thing about Armless Tiger Man," Lando said.

"What is it? No, don't tell me. I can't take anymore. What is it?"

He narrowed his eyes at me from under his mask. "Armless Tiger Man and Captain America are mortal enemies."

"Of course, they are!" I cried. "Captain America is like this great hero and Armless Tiger Man is a disgusting Nazi."

Just then Mrs. Hill walked into the room. "Aven, sweetie, come with me."

I followed her down the hall to a closet. She opened it.

"Whoa," I said. It was crammed with about a hundred costumes.

"I know we can make something new out of the stuff in here," Mrs. Hill said, adjusting her wig, her eyes full of determination. She scratched at her green chin. "Did you read about the Armless Master in your, uh, research?" She asked as she pulled out a green cape.

"No, I just saw Armless Tiger Man."

She pulled out a flesh colored foamy muscle suit. "Well, if we take this green Loki cape and combine it with this Sumo suit . . . "

"Sumo suit?" I asked.

She waved a hand in the air. "Don't ask. Experiment gone wrong." She draped the cape over my shoulders. "Yes, I think you could be the Armless Master. He's pretty tough."

I smiled at her, but the corners of my mouth shook and my eyes filled with tears. "Oh, honey," Mrs. Hill said, wrapping her arms around me and pulling my head into her foamy chest. "It's okay."

"I'm sorry," I sobbed into the foam. "I can't believe how stupid I am. I didn't mean to dress like a Nazi."

She ran a hand over my head as I cried. "Of course, you didn't. No one thinks that. And you are definitely not stupid, Aven."

"Yes, I am." I pulled away. "I swear I don't like Nazis," I sobbed, tears running down my cheeks. "I hate them. I really, really hate them."

Mrs. Hill put her hands on my shoulders and gripped them. "I really, really know that." She smiled and wiped at my cheeks. "Are you okay, honey?"

I sniffled. "I will be."

Mrs. Hill nodded. Then she picked up the flesh-colored foam suit and held it up to me. "Now let's see . . . I think I'll need to tailor this just a bit. It won't be the best, but I can pull it together pretty quickly."

All this anger.
All this fear.
It's been building.
You're about to hear.

—Kids from Alcatraz

AND MRS. HILL AMAZINGLY DID
pull it together. My costume ended up looking pretty
good, though I wondered if people would know who I
was. Mr. Hill, all decked out in his killer Black Lightning
costume with actual glowing blue lightning bolts on his
chest, drove us all in the van.

"You know," Mr. Hill said, "you could have dressed her
up as Arm-Fall-Off-Boy. That would have been a good one."

I gaped at Mr. Hill in the rearview mirror. "Arm-
Fall-Off-Boy? You've got to be joking?"

"That can't be real," Connor said. "Then again, I
wouldn't think Armless Tiger Man or the Armless Master could be real either."

"That's a complicated costume," Mrs. Hill said. "I don't think I could have pulled it off so quickly."

"You're right," Mr. Hill said. "You couldn't pull it off. At least, not like Arm-Fall-Off-Boy pulls his own arms off." Mr. Hill was clearly impressed at his joke as he grinned at all of us in the rearview mirror.

We all sort of half-groaned, half-giggled. "Maybe next year," I said.

"Dude!" A guy in a Joker costume said as he walked by Lando and me. "The Armless Master! That's so rad!"

I smiled at Lando as the Joker walked off. We had already lost Connor and Zion to a video gaming exhibit and Mr. and Mrs. Hill to a panel on intersectional feminism in comics. "I guess people do recognize me," I said.

"Yeah, you're pretty memorable," Lando said, smiling.

"*Whoa.*" A storm trooper stopped in front of me. "Are you the Armless Master?" he asked from under his helmet.

"Yep."

"How'd you make it look so real?" the Storm Trooper asked, circling me. "How'd you hide your arms like that?"

"Chainsaw," I told him.

He stood there a moment before saying, "Huh?"

"I take Comic Con very seriously."

"What?"

"I'm a hardcore method actor."

The Storm Trooper backed away from me. "I almost believe you."

Lando chuckled beside me as the Storm Trooper left. I felt kind of bad about traumatizing him, so when the next person asked me how I made my armlessness look so real, I told her it was CGI.

"Comic Con is awesome," I said, looking around at all the nerds. I wished every place could be like this. Only with better smells.

A couple of guys about my age in Wolverine and Cyclops costumes walked by us. Wolverine gave me the horrible "I can't stop staring at you because you're a freak" look.

I stared right back at him. "What are you looking at, Wolverine?"

There seemed to be something about being in costume at Comic Con that made me feel way bolder than usual. Like I was someone else.

And I was sick to death of people looking at me like those guys did.

"Nothing," Wolverine said, walking away with

Cyclops. But I could hear him say to his friend as he walked away, "That was freaky."

My heart pounded. I felt like all my anger that had been building over the last couple of weeks was about to explode. And it did. "You know what's freaky?" I said, stomping after the X-Men. "Wolverine with giant sweat stains!"

The two guys turned around. "Huh?" said Wolverine.

"Yeah, you heard me, nerd boy!" I exclaimed loud enough that several people around us had stopped what they were doing and watched us. "Wolverine is not a geek with sweat stains! And a perm! Wolverine most certainly does not have a perm!"

Several people around us giggled as I felt Lando's arm slip around my waist from behind and start pulling me away. Wolverine's face scrunched up in anger. "My hair is naturally curly!" he squealed. "Naturally curly! All natural!"

"Yeah, I bet those sweat stains are natural, too!" I cried as Lando snorted behind me but kept pulling me back.

"It's over a hundred degrees outside!" Wolverine waved his rubber claws at me.

"Why are you picking a fight, Armless Master?" Cyclops said. "You want a go?"

I squirmed in Lando's arms. "Oh, yeah, I want a go! I'll take you both down. Don't you know who I am? I'll Kung Fu you both!"

And then the people around us were chanting, "Armless Master. Armless Master."

Zion and Connor ran up to us, their eyes wide. "Aven, you're going to get us in trouble," Lando said.

I walked away with my friends, my chest puffed out. "No one better mess with me today."

"I don't think anyone else will," Lando mumbled. He smiled and shook his head, walking off to check out a Harry Potter display.

"I can't believe you did that," Zion scolded me and then ran off to join his brother—like they both needed to put distance between themselves and me.

I turned to Connor. "You got something to say, huh? Bring it on!"

Connor barked, clucked his tongue, blinked his eyes. I had clearly stressed him out, and I felt kind of bad about that. "Need anger management much, Aven? What is *up* with you?"

"Those guys were being rude."

"People are rude all the time, and you don't normally react like that."

"Well, I couldn't take it today."

"Why not?"

"I just couldn't."

Connor stared at me and shrugged. "You've been acting so weird the last couple of weeks. You won't answer my calls, you're no fun to hang out with—"

"Hey!"

"And you just flipped out at Comic Con."

I took a deep breath and willed my temper to cool off. "I'm sorry," I said. "I'm having a hard time."

"With what?"

"With stupid school. High school sucks. I haven't even made any friends since I started."

"It's only been a few weeks. And you have Zion."

"Maybe I want more friends. Is that too much to ask?"

"It seems like Lando's your friend."

I glanced over at Lando. "Yeah, I guess. But that's different. He hangs out with other people at school. And he's, like, cool."

"And I guess you're not cool."

I snorted. "I'm definitely not cool."

"And why is that bad?" When I didn't answer, Connor said, "I'm not cool either, you know. And Zion's not cool. None of us are cool, Aven. But you know what? I'm okay with that. Aren't you?"

"Not when it makes people treat me like garbage."

"Who's treating you like garbage?"

I stared down at my yellow flip-flops.

"I see. More secrets."

Zion and Lando walked back to us, and Lando aimed a wand at my head and tapped it on my frazzled red hair. "*Calm downus!*" He grinned.

"I am calm," I said. "I'm not going to get us into trouble."

"That was pretty tough, though," Lando said. "I think those guys were seriously scared."

"What can I say? I'm pretty scary."

"You *are* scary," Zion said. "For real."

"Yeah, 'cause I'll for real kick your butt," I said.

Zion watched me warily as he and Lando walked back over to the Harry Potter exhibit. Lando turned around and mouthed the word *scary*, then smiled. I smiled back and shook my head at him.

I turned and found Connor watching me. "You *like* him," Connor said.

"What? Like who?"

"Lando."

"Of course, I like him. He's Zion's brother."

"No, I mean you *like* him, like him."

"What? I do not." My cheeks felt like they were

going to melt off. I wasn't sure if it was from my fight with Wolverine or from Connor's accusations.

Connor shrugged. "I mean, it's okay if you do. I would understand." But Connor didn't make eye contact with me. He stared at the ground and fiddled with the dog fur on his costume. He clucked his tongue a few times.

"Well, I don't," I said. "At least not like you like *Amanda*." I instantly regretted saying that.

Connor looked up at me. "What?"

"Nothing."

"I don't like her like that. She's just a friend."

"Well, I don't like anyone like that, and I doubt I ever will."

Connor frowned. "Why?"

"Because no one would ever like me like that."

Connor opened his mouth like he might say something, but I turned around and pushed my way through the crowd of characters before he could see the tears in my eyes.

*Life is hard
And hardly ever fair.*

—Llama Parade

"I CAN'T BELIEVE WE'RE GOING TO homecoming," Zion whined as he sadly took a bite of his sandwich.

"I can't believe it either." I swung my bag onto the lunch table and eased my head out from under it. I sunk down in my chair. "Like I said . . ." I leaned forward and whispered, "Y. M. C. A."

I glanced over at Lando's table and saw him laugh about something. I'm not sure why I made a special note of the fact that he and Janessa weren't sitting next to each other. Connor's words echoed in my head. *You like* him*, like* him. Lando looked over at our table and waved at me. I quickly turned away from him.

"So Comic Con was fun," I said casually.

"Yeah, it was okay," Zion said.

"I'd totally go again next year."

"As long as you don't start any more fights."

"I didn't start the fight." I stuck my chin out. "I ended it."

"Yeah, about ended up in jail."

I snorted. "You're such an exaggerator." I sat there for a moment. "What do you think they would do about my fingerprints if I went to jail?"

"I guess they'd have to print your toes."

"Cool," I said. "I kind of wish I *had* ended up in jail."

I opened my bag and pulled out my pretzels. I popped one in my mouth as a smarmy voice behind me said, "Leave some food for the rest of us, Lardon."

Zion stared down at his sandwich, all crawled back into himself. I could see what Joshua was starting to do to him again—the power he had over him. I wondered how much of Zion's terrible shyness and insecurity about his weight was because of Joshua. My heart pounded with anger.

"You like your finger foods, don't you, Aven?" Joshua went on. "Or would those be toe foods for you?"

Was I going to let him have that same power over me?

I whirled around to face him. "I do like toe foods," I said. "Just not as much as you like butt foods."

"That doesn't even make any sense," Joshua said.

"It makes sense to people with half a brain."

"And apparently to people with half a body." Joshua laughed at his own stupid joke. I glared at him, willing my eyes to not fill with tears as he joined his friends at their table.

I turned around and slumped in my chair.

"Maybe you were right," Zion said.

"About what?"

"Maybe we should eat outside."

I shook my head. "I am not going to let that guy beat us." I leaned forward. "And you're not going to let him do this to you. We shouldn't care at all what he says or does."

But I could see that Zion cared. And as much as I tried to deny it, I cared too—so much that when a kid burst into the cafeteria and screamed, "It's raining!" Zion and I just sat at our table, sadly glancing at each other while everything around us erupted into chaos. Kids pushed past one another, laughing and screaming and grabbing and shoving, in their eagerness to get a small sprinkle of cool desert rain on their faces.

Zion and I just focused on making it through lunch.

The air had slightly cooled for a few hours as a result of the sprinkle we'd had, and it smelled amazing at

Stagecoach Pass as I walked through the park that day after school. There was nothing quite like the smell of the desert after a rain. Too bad it had to come with humidity, making my clothes feel sticky.

I sat next to Spaghetti in the shaded covering of the petting zoo and rubbed his soft fur with my foot. He barely acknowledged me. "He's still so sluggish," I told Denise. "Has he been eating?"

"A little," Denise said as she filled the water troughs with a hose. "It's still so darn hot. I wish that rain had lasted longer. How could anyone act spry in this muggy weather?"

I shrugged. I had to admit I felt sluggish myself, like I could crawl in bed and sleep for, oh, the next four years.

"I wish I were a llama," I said to Denise. "Then I could live here in the petting zoo and not have to worry about anything."

"But what if you didn't live in a petting zoo?" Denise said. "Then you'd have plenty to worry about."

"Like what?"

"Like getting eaten by a mountain lion."

"That's why I would be a petting zoo llama. They live a life of leisure."

At least my career options were growing: hermit, llama.

Denise smiled. "I suppose. But it seems kind of boring to me."

I saw Trilby walking by. "Trilby!" I called out, but she didn't seem to hear me. "Trilby!" I cried again. "Trilby!"

She finally looked over. She waved and pulled an ear bud out of her ear. She made her way into the petting zoo and sat down in the dirt beside Spaghetti and me. "You have to hear this new band I just discovered," she said. "They're called We Are Librarians." She laughed. "Isn't that awesome?"

I smiled as she put the bud in my ear, and I tried not to think about how we were sharing ear wax. I sat there listening to We Are Librarians in one ear while Trilby went on about how excited she was to go to homecoming with Zion and me in the other ear. She rubbed her hands all over Spaghetti while she talked, and I thought if anyone could pep him up, it would be Trilby. But still he sat there all lifeless.

"I better get back," Trilby said. "I was just enjoying the smell of the rain."

"I'll walk with you," I told her.

While we walked, I told Trilby how Dad couldn't believe that her dad was in a punk band because he'd once seen him wear a polo shirt, which she thought was hilarious. "They still get together and play every now and then but not often. You know, I don't think you can ever turn it off."

"Turn what off?" I asked.

"The love of playing music," she said. "I think my dad will still rock out even when he's super old."

"Have you ever thought about starting a band?" I asked her.

She stopped and grabbed me, like this was the most serious subject ever. "All. The. Time."

I looked shyly down at me feet. "I, uh, play the guitar a little."

"What?" Trilby practically screamed right in face. "How could I not already know this? We have to start a band, Aven. We *have* to."

"I don't think I can do that," I said, still looking down at the ground. "I can't perform in front of people."

"Why not?"

I looked up at her. "I like to keep a low profile."

Trilby frowned. "I think it's time for you to start keeping a high profile."

I smiled. "I'll think about it."

Trilby threw her head back and groaned. "Man, that's what people always say when they mean no. Like when I ask my parents if I can open a chicken sanctuary.

They always say 'We'll think about it.' Do I have a chicken sanctuary?" She crossed her arms. "Nope."

"You kind of have a thing for chickens, don't you?" I said.

"Have you ever seen them wearing pants?"

I giggled. "No."

Trilby narrowed her eyes. "I strongly suggest Stagecoach Pass puts all the chickens in the petting zoo in pants. I predict attendance will go up by . . ." she scratched at her chin. "Twenty percent at least."

I giggled again. "I'll suggest it to my parents."

I left Trilby at Sonoran Smoothies and went to visit Chili. She reached her head down to my foot when I walked into her stall. "Smart girl," I whispered as I slipped my foot out of my flip-flop and rubbed at her head. Then I laid my body against her side, feeling her breath. "We have to figure out how to work together," I told her. "I know I'm a different kind of rider. But we have to figure this all out. I don't want to give up on you." I stood back. "And I don't want you to give up on me."

Chili didn't seem nearly as worried about the horse show as I was. I wished I could be so carefree. Being a horse must have been amazing.

I decided to check on Henry. I couldn't stop thinking about him growing up in orphanages. And those things he said about the nuns hitting him with a brush—it all made me so sad. I wondered what he had been like as a kid. He was so old, it was tough to imagine him as any kind of kid at all. I kept picturing a three-foot tall Henry with wrinkles and white hair.

He was busy talking to a woman at the counter when I walked in. I sat down at a table and waited while he sold her some saltwater taffy, then she left the store.

Henry smiled when he saw me. "Hi, Aven."

"Hi, Henry."

"Would you like some ice cream?"

I stood up and walked to the counter. "How about a scoop of mint chip?" I said. I didn't care if he got it wrong today.

He nodded and picked up the scoop. I watched as he struggled to get ice cream into the scooper—like he didn't have the strength to do it. Then he dropped the ball of ice cream on the floor before he could get it in the bowl. He went to grab a rag, and I saw how his hands shook.

I walked around behind the counter. "Go sit down, Henry. I'll clean this up."

He nodded and shakily walked out of the store. For a moment I was worried he was going to wander off. I'd heard about old people with memory problems walking off and getting lost. But I saw he sat down in one of the rocking chairs.

I worked at cleaning up the ice cream mess on the floor and dumped the rags in the sink. Then I went out and sat next to Henry in a rocking chair on the porch. "Are you okay?" I asked him.

He nodded. "I'm tired." He rocked gently. "Just really tired."

We rocked in silence awhile until I asked him, "How long were you an orphan, Henry?"

He stared out at the park. "All my life."

"No one ever adopted you?"

He rubbed at his wrinkled forehead then ran an age-spotted hand over his white hair. "No. No, I guess I wasn't lucky like you."

I smiled, glad he remembered who I was, though it was getting later in the day.

"Where did you go grow up?"

"In an orphanage, of course. Back then we had to go to orphanages. That was . . . a long time ago. Nineteen thirties when I was born. There was the Depression. Lots of kids went into orphanages."

"But where was your orphanage?"

"Mostly in Chicago," he said.

"Was that the Angel Guardian orphanage you mentioned?"

"Yeah, that one. And others."

"So were you born in Chicago?"

"I don't know. I was shuffled around a lot. Not sure. I tried getting my paperwork once, but no one could find it for me."

"You don't remember having a family ever?"

"Nope. Must've been too young to remember when I went in. Don't even know what happened to my parents."

"So you *could* have brothers or sisters then," I said, mostly to myself.

Henry shrugged. "I suppose. But it's been so long. I wouldn't have the slightest idea how to find them. And they might be dead." He rubbed at his forehead. "I don't want to talk about this anymore."

"Okay."

That night I searched for all I could find about Chicago orphanages in the 1930s. It was difficult to find any good information about them. There were thousands of children in Chicago orphanages in the 1940s, over 1,200 of them in Angel Guardian alone.

What I did find, however, were lots and lots of people on message boards trying to locate their records, trying to figure out who they were, where they'd come from, and if they had any other family. There were people on there looking for brothers and sisters who they'd been separated from—a woman searching for her older sister, another woman trying to find her three little brothers, and a man searching for his younger sister and baby brother, who'd be about Henry's age by now. My heart sunk when I saw the post was already over ten years old.

There were also stories of abuse—of growing up in a world where no one cared about them or wanted them. Had Henry grown up like that? No matter what was happening in my life, at least I knew there were people in this world who cared about me. I went to bed that night, my heart broken for Henry. And for all the people searching for their lost family members.

How can I make it through tomorrow
When I can't make it through tonight?
How can I make it through tonight
When I have no more fight?

—Kids from Alcatraz

THE DAY OF THE HOMECOMING football game, after Zion and I watched about ten videos of chickens in pants at his house (Trilby was right—attendance would definitely go up by at *least* twenty percent), we worked on some more guitar lessons together. "No, that's the wrong chord," I told Zion. "You're supposed to be playing A Major."

"I was."

"No, you were playing C Major."

Zion adjusted his fingers. "See, A Major."

"Well, *now* you're playing A Major."

"I can't concentrate," Zion said. "I can't believe you did this to me."

"Did what?"

"Asked Trilby to go to homecoming."

"Everything is going to be fine," I assured him. "Trilby wouldn't have agreed to go with you if she didn't want to."

"I never would have asked her in the first place."

"Which is why I needed to step in. This is good for you. You're getting out. Breaking out of your comfort zone."

Zion glared at me. "And what are you doing, hermit wannabe?"

"I'm assisting you in making it happen."

"No, I mean what are you doing to break out of your comfort zone and move on?"

"Well, I'm going to the dance, too, aren't I?"

"What else are you doing?"

"I'm teaching you how to play the guitar." I turned my attention back to Zion's hands. "Now try playing D Major."

"I don't know why you waste your time, Aven," Lando said, standing in the doorway. "Dude will always be terrible."

"He's not terrible," I insisted.

Zion glared at Lando. "Get out of here."

Lando stepped into the room. "Worst guitar player of all time."

"Get out or I'll tell Ma."

Instead of leaving, Lando plopped down on the bed next to us. Zion looked like he might be having an aneurysm. He shot up and threw the guitar down on the bed. "I'm telling Ma!"

Lando and I giggled as Zion stormed out of the room. "Tattletale!" Lando called after him. In the other room we could hear Zion whining to their mom.

"He's trying," I said. "Go easy on him."

"I just wanted to get him out of here."

My stomach twisted up into a knot. "Why?"

"Because I want you to play that song you were playing last time."

I swallowed. "What song?"

"I don't know. It was like some old song."

I tried to think—a serious challenge with Lando staring at me like this. "Oh, you mean 'Free Fallin'?"

His face lit up. "Yeah, I think that's it." He picked up the guitar and laid it at my feet.

I hoped he didn't notice my shaking toes as I tried to remember how to play the stupid song. I started strumming.

"No." Lando shook his head.

I stopped strumming. "What?"

"You have to sing it."

"I don't sing."

"Yes, you do. I heard you."

"I was only singing because I didn't realize you were *spying* on me."

"Will you sing if I go stand outside the doorway then?"

I smiled and bit down on my lip. "No."

"So you won't dance and you won't sing."

I shook my head. "No," I whispered.

"Why not?"

I went back to gently strumming the guitar. "I don't know." But I lied. I knew exactly why. I was too ashamed to admit that I was afraid of what other people would think of me.

I stopped playing the song when I realized Lando was staring down at me. I slowly raised my head and met his eyes. "You do know," he said. "And your reason is stupid."

His words hit me like a punch to the forehead. What did he care anyway? I opened my mouth to say as much, but Zion stormed back into the room. "Ma says to get out and leave us alone."

Lando stood up. "No problem. I've got to get ready to go anyway."

"Yeah, that's what I thought," Zion said, giving

his brother a dirty look as he left the room. Then he sat down on the bed beside me and picked the guitar back up. "I don't know why he's bugging us anyway," he mumbled.

I stared at the guitar. "I don't know either."

"I like your shirt today," I told Mr. Hill as we all piled into the van that evening.

He looked down at his Avengers T-shirt with Nick Fury on it. "Thank you, Aven."

"How did he lose his eye?" I asked from the back seat.

"There are multiple theories. With the original white Nick Fury, it was believed he lost it from a grenade blast in World War Two," Mr. Hill explained. "But the new black Nick Fury was written to have lost it during the Gulf War when he was ambushed while transporting Wolverine through Kuwait."

"Interesting," I said. Mr. Hill was like a comic book encyclopedia.

"They rewrite characters and backstories all the time," Mr. Hill said.

We pulled into the school parking lot, and Lando jumped out and ran off carrying his football gear. Zion and I went to find seats while Mr. and Mrs. Hill waited in line to get drinks and snacks for us. We walked up the bleacher steps past lots of kids from school. And then there was Janessa.

I guess it was because she was Lando's girlfriend and Zion was one of my best friends and we would all be going to homecoming together the next day that I summoned my courage and stopped in front of her. "Hi, Janessa," I said, giving her the biggest smile I could muster. "Are you excited for the game?"

She literally didn't even respond—just sat there with her friends, looking at us like Zion was a giant booger with arms and legs, and I was a giant booger with legs.

Why someone else being rude to me should have made me feel so incredibly embarrassed, I honestly didn't know. But I felt . . . ashamed. And the only thing I could have felt ashamed of at that moment was myself. And I felt ashamed that I let her make me feel ashamed. If that made sense.

I hurried up the steps behind Zion, who had taken off the moment she'd looked at us like we were festering zits.

We found an open spot and sat down. "She's awful," Zion breathed. "I don't know why Lando likes her."

I thought about Janessa's perfect long brown hair

and face and the fact that she had *all* her body parts. "I know why," I said.

Mr. and Mrs. Hill made their way up to us as the game was starting, but I didn't feel like eating the popcorn and nachos they'd bought for us.

"Maybe you could all go to the dance tomorrow without me," I said to Zion as I watched Joshua down on the field. Then my eyes moved to Janessa several rows below us.

Zion shook his head. "You're not backing out on this—not because of stupid Janessa."

"It's not because of her. I mean, it's partly because of her. We do have to drive to homecoming with her and Lando."

"She acts nicer when Lando's there."

I snorted. "Hardly."

Zion popped a nacho into his mouth and then offered them to me. I shook my head. "Don't worry, you'll get through tomorrow," he said.

I looked once more down at the field where Joshua stood. "I have to get through today first."

Zion shrugged and chewed on another nacho. "One day at a time."

Run away
Or become a bot.
Run away.
Change your thought.

—The Square Pegs

I PUT ON MY PURPLE TANK DRESS and slip-on Star Wars Vans. I guess I'd gotten swept up in the Hill family's passion for Star Wars when I'd picked them. My shoulders slumped as I gazed at myself in the mirror and realized I'd put my dress on backward. There went fifteen minutes of my life down the toilet.

Mom helped me with my makeup so I didn't have to go the stupid dance all smudgy. "They're going to play the 'Y.M.C.A.,' Mom," I told her as she brushed my lids with eye shadow. "I'll be humiliated."

"Don't be ridiculous, honey. You're going to have a blast. She blew on my lids. "And if they play the 'Y.M.C.A.,' go get something to drink until it's over."

"People will make fun of me."

"I don't think so."

"They will. You don't know how mean they can be."

She stopped and stared at me, like she was waiting for me to tell her what I meant. And I almost told her right then and there about my Great Humiliation, but when I opened my mouth, nothing came out. She would be horrified. She would cry. It would be emotional. And I couldn't get all emotional while she was putting mascara on my pale red lashes.

She put the mascara back in the makeup bag and broke out the blush. My head shot back. "Are you serious?"

She nodded. "Yeah, you're probably right." She snapped the blush shut and took out the tube of lip gloss. "Why do you even have blush?" she asked as she swiped my lips with the light glossy color.

"It came with a set."

"Can I have it?"

"Be my guest."

"There," she said, studying my face. "You're beautiful."

I turned and gazed at myself in the bathroom mirror. "Whoa," I said. "It looks so much better when you do it. Are you available for full-time hire?"

"Nope," she said. "Only for special occasions."

I grimaced. "Is this a special occasion?"

"Of course, it is." She covered her mouth with her hands. "My baby's going to her first dance."

"I wish I were as excited as you are, Mom." I hopped down from the bathroom counter, and we walked out to the living room together.

Dad whistled when he saw me. "My, aren't you perty, little lady," he said in a southern accent.

There was a knock on the door, and Mom opened it to let Trilby in. She wore a cute pink baby doll dress and now had pink streaks in her short blonde hair. "Trilby!" I cried, and she hugged me.

"How do you do those cute streaks in your hair?" I asked her.

"Hair chalk!" she announced. She opened up her cross-shoulder bag and pulled out a handful of hair chalks. "I have purple, too. I should do yours. It would match your dress!"

We sat on the couch, and as Trilby worked on putting purple streaks in my red hair, I said, "It's really nice that you agreed to go to the dance with Zion."

"I'm excited to go. No one's ever asked me to go to a dance before. And he's so sweet."

I smiled at her. "He is sweet. I'm glad you think so."

"Have you discovered any new bands you like?" she asked me as she picked up a long strand of my red hair.

"I like We Are Librarians."

"Oh my gosh!" Trilby exclaimed. "'Banned Book' is already one of my favorite songs ever."

"I'll add that one to my playlist."

When Trilby was done, I went to the bathroom to check myself out. "You like?" she asked from behind me.

I nodded. I did like. I liked it very much.

"We're going to go wait outside for Zion," I told Mom and Dad as Trilby and I attempted to escape.

"Not until we get pictures," Mom said excitedly. "But outside's a good idea. Better lighting."

We all four walked down the steps from the apartment while my parents debated whether to take the pictures in front of the saguaro cactus near the entrance, the line of palo verde trees by the parking lot, or the great big mesquite tree in the center of the park.

We decided to go out to the parking lot. Trilby was taking a picture of me with my parents as Mrs. Hill pulled up. Mom walked over to the car to say hi. "Zion, why don't you get out so we can get a picture of you and Trilby?"

I thought Zion's eyes were going to pop out of his

head when he saw Trilby. "Hi, Zion," she said, but he looked around awkwardly. And then when she put her arm around him for pictures, he seemed like he was struggling to breathe. I worried he might pass out.

Everyone else got out of the van, and I noticed that Lando's friend Justin was with him. Not Janessa.

Lando stood next me and planted one foot next to mine. "We have the same kicks."

I looked down at our matching Star Wars Vans. Then I grinned up at Lando. "I guess you didn't realize you were buying girl shoes, huh?"

Lando laughed. "Check the sizing. They're men's."

I smiled. "Yeah, I know."

Lando punched me lightly on the shoulder. "Why are you so cool, Aven?"

And then I was the one struggling to breathe. "I'm not," I mumbled, which seemed to disappoint Lando. Then I was mad at myself for acting stupid as Lando turned his attention to Justin.

"Where's Janessa?" I whispered to Zion.

"She and Lando broke up."

"Why?"

Zion gave me a look like he couldn't understand why I was interested. I wasn't entirely sure myself why I was so interested. "I don't care," he said. "Good riddance."

We took about a hundred more pictures of all of us before we piled back into the van. Zion, Trilby, and I sat quietly in the back row until I couldn't stop myself from asking the question. "Where's Janessa? I thought she was coming with us."

Zion mouthed at me, "I told you."

Lando shrugged. "I don't care. Ma never liked her anyway, so it's all good."

"I did so like Janessa," Mrs. Hill insisted.

"You did not," Lando said. "You said she was shallow."

"Oh, well, yes, she was," Mrs. Hill said. "She was definitely that."

Mrs. Hill dropped us off near the gym around seven o'clock and told us she'd be back by eleven. I couldn't believe we had to be at this dance for four hours.

"If you wanted to come back at eight, that would be okay, too, Mom," Zion said. I nodded in agreement.

Trilby laughed. "No way! I want to dance!"

"You guys are going to have so much fun," Mrs. Hill assured us.

The five of us walked into the gym together, and it wasn't long before Justin and Lando found their friends and went off.

Zion, Trilby, and I sat in chairs over in a corner as

far away from where everyone was dancing as possible. We sat there awkwardly until the 'Y.M.C.A.' came on. "I told you," I said to Zion.

He put up his hands. "Hey, I didn't make them play it."

"You didn't have to. It's automatic. Like an automatic school dance requirement."

"I want to do it," Trilby whined. "Come on, Zion. Why'd we come here if we aren't going to dance?"

Zion's eyes darted around. "People will see us."

Trilby jumped up from her chair. "Who cares?" Then she grabbed Zion and pulled him onto the dance floor.

"I can't leave Aven," Zion said.

Trilby stopped and looked at me like she was asking for my permission.

"Yes, you can," I said. "Please go dance."

And then they left me. Sitting in a chair in the corner. All alone. I spotted Joshua's group not far away. I got up and walked through the dancing crowds to another part of the gym and sat down on a bleacher.

Thankfully the 'Y.M.C.A.' ended and another slower song came on. I sat there in my cheap purple dress and all my stupid makeup and purple hair chalk and my favorite shoes surrounded by dancing, laughing high schoolers. I wanted to cry.

I wished Connor were here. I wondered what he was

doing right then. Was he hanging out with Amanda? The thought made me want to cry even more.

Lando seemed to appear from nowhere and sat down beside me. "What are you doing sitting here all by yourself?"

"Zion and Trilby are dancing." I bit the inside of my cheek and willed my eyes to stay dry.

We sat there for a while, Lando tapping his Star Wars Vans on the bleachers to the beat of the song. "You look pretty, you know," he said.

I turned to him, not sure I'd heard him right with the loud music. "Huh?"

He smiled and said louder, "You look pretty." He picked up a strand of my hair then dropped it. "I like the purple."

I didn't know what to say. Why would he say that to me? What was he doing?

"Do you want to dance with me?" he asked me then. I stared at him, but he smiled. Then he laughed. "Can you hear anything I'm saying to you?"

"Why?"

"Because you won't answer me."

"No, I mean why are you asking me to dance?"

Lando scrunched up his eyebrows. "Why does a person usually ask another person to dance?"

"Why?"

"So they can dance!"

Just then Joshua walked by us and blew me a kiss. And Lando saw it. "What was that all about?" he asked me.

I shook my head.

Don't cry don't cry don't cry.

Was high school going to be four long years of me trying not to cry?

"Why did he do that?"

I kept shaking my head, my throat too constricted to speak. I couldn't hold it in any longer. I jumped up and ran through the crowded gym until I got to the door. I banged my hip against the handlebar so hard it would probably bruise later and burst through into the warm night air.

I ran along the sidewalk until I reached the empty football field. I ran up the concrete steps, stumbling on one, scraping my knee and twisting my ankle. "*Ouch*," I groaned, sitting down on a bleacher. I rolled my ankle around and pain shot through it. "No," I said quietly to myself as a tear ran down my cheek. That last thing I needed was to hurt my foot.

I sat there on the bleacher overlooking the empty field. There were no sounds except for a few crickets chirping. I realized I was sitting in nearly the same exact spot where Janessa had sat the day before—when she'd looked at me like I was something she'd found between her toes. Janessa with her perfect hair (mine looked like I traveled exclusively via roller coaster); her perfect makeup (unlike my uneven everything); her perfect clothes (non-name brand clearance rack for me); and her perfectly manicured nails.

I heard approaching footsteps and then a soft voice below me say my name. I stayed quiet, not wanting Lando to know I was sitting here crying by myself like some weirdo in the middle of the empty bleachers. I considered diving to the ground and lying flat until he left.

"Aven, I can see you up there," he said.

I attempted to wipe my wet cheeks on my shoulders as he walked up the steps to where I sat. I hoped my makeup wasn't running down my face. Then again, it would be hard to tell in the dark.

Lando sat down next to me. "Why'd you run off like that? Was it Joshua?"

I shook my head. "I didn't feel well."

"Like how you didn't feel well at the mall?"

"What do you mean?"

"I mean why don't you say what's going on instead of hiding?"

"I'm not hiding," I said, thinking about how I'd just considered diving under the bleachers. *To hide.* "I get claustrophobic in places with a lot of people."

"Why did Joshua blow a kiss at you?"

"Why did Janessa break up with you?"

"Nope. Answer my question first."

"Because he's a jerk. Now answer my question."

"She didn't. I broke up with her."

I stared at him. "Why?"

"Because she's a jerk."

"What did she do?"

He shrugged. "Nothing specific. Sometimes she would just say something about someone that would rub me the wrong way."

"Like what?"

"Like . . . mean stuff."

"About Zion?"

"Sometimes." I knew he was looking at me, though I could barely make out his eyes in the dark. He shook his head. "But we don't need to go into it."

I stared down at my hurt foot. "We don't have to. I can guess what kinds of things she said."

"Like I said, she's a jerk."

I turned my ankle around and grimaced. "A pretty jerk."

"*Nah*," Lando said. "She wasn't so pretty to me after a while, you know? Like the ugliness inside starts to spread to the outside."

I thought about how I'd thought Joshua was so cute when I'd first seen him. Now the look of him made me feel sick. "Yeah, I know." I put my foot down and tried to press a little weight on it. I grunted in pain.

"You do something to your foot?"

I nodded as I tried to turn my ankle again. "I twisted it when I walked up the steps." More like sprinted up the steps. No, more like *teleported* up the steps.

"Here, let me see." Before I could stop him, he picked up my foot and set it on his lap. He removed my shoe, and I prayed fervently my foot didn't stink.

Lando squeezed around my tender ankle, but it felt like he was squeezing my heart instead. I tried to take slow steady breaths as he wrapped his hands around my ankle and put pressure on it. My chest felt like a hummingbird was flying around in it. "How's that feel?"

"It hurts, but I think it will be okay."

He frowned. "You scraped your knee, too." He reached up like he might touch my knee, but I threw my leg down before he could. "It's fine. I'm fine."

I grabbed my shoe from him with my toes and tossed it on the ground in front of me. I slipped my foot in and shot up from the bleachers. "I gotta go," I said and started limping down the steps.

Lando stood. "Where are you going?"

"I gotta go home," I called back.

"But we're your ride!"

"I gotta go find Zion." I didn't look back at Lando as I got to the sidewalk and ran away as fast as my throbbing ankle would allow.

I'm such a hypocrite.
Can't take my own advice.
I deserve what's coming
And it won't be nice.

—Screaming Ferret

JOSEPHINE AND I SAT IN THE CAFETERIA
eating turkey and gravy and mashed potatoes over
white bread. Josephine was right—the food at Golden
Sunset was mediocre at best.

"So if you like someone . . . theoretically, of course—"

"Like someone?" Josephine interrupted me.

"Yeah, I mean *like* them, like them."

"Who do you like?"

I rolled my eyes and stabbed a piece of turkey with
the fork I held in my toes. "No one. I told you. It's
theoretical."

"Is it that boy you told me about?"

"Oh my gosh. You're so not listening to me." I

shoved the dry turkey into my mouth and gulped it. "What part of theoretical do you not understand? And I told you—that boy's a jerk. Anyway, it doesn't matter. I don't know why I try to talk to you about stuff."

"Well, I don't know why either if you're going to be all snippy about it."

We sat there quietly for a while, the sounds of silverware clanking against dishes all around us. Every now and then some old guy would make a loud hacking cough like he'd nearly choked to death on the dry turkey. Josephine kept glancing at me then quickly looking away all casually like she didn't care that I was there.

"So," I said. "Let's just say that you like someone who's cute and popular and everyone likes him and he could never like you back. How would you shut it off?"

Josephine stared at me. "Shut it off?"

"Yeah, you know. Shut the feelings off. Shut them down. Like shut them *down*. Way, way down. Push them down into the deepest pit on earth."

"Really?" she said. "You're still going to be making fun of my book like that?"

"Did you ever finish it? Did the dude turn into a pirate fossil after all?" Josephine ignored me and sipped her water. "No, I'm serious, though. I mean, how do you do it?"

"Do what exactly?"

"Shut your feelings off, you know, for boys?"

Josephine scowled. "Why would you think I'd know how to do that?"

"Because you never have a boyfriend or anything. You said you never had time for that nonsense."

Josephine huffed and stuffed a bite of turkey in her mouth. "I've liked boys before."

"No, I don't believe it. You've never liked anyone."

"Well, I didn't conjure your mama out of thin air, you know!"

My curiosity was definitely piqued with that statement. "So who was he?"

"Who?"

"My old grandpa!"

Josephine chuckled. "Nobody."

"Was he a handsome cowboy you met down in Texas? Did he wear spurs and have manly stubble? Did he smell like leather and cow pies?"

Josephine was laughing now. "No, he did not smell like cow pies at all."

"Then who was he?"

"He was a soldier," she said. "And he was killed in Vietnam."

My smile fell. "Oh," I whispered.

Josephine waved a hand in the air. "It was a long time ago."

I stared at her as she drummed her fingers on the peach linen tablecloth. "So did you like him?" I asked.

She smiled down at the table. "Yes, I did." She sniffed. "Very much."

"And you haven't liked anyone since?"

She shrugged. "Alone with a baby . . . Like I said, I never again had time for that nonsense."

We sat there quietly until I saw Milford sit down at a table near ours. He waved at us. "You have plenty of time on your hands now," I said to Josephine.

She looked over at Milford and snorted. "What? For him? No, thank you."

"Why not? He's kind of cute in a wrinkled, old man way."

Milford's smile grew by about 200 percent when he noticed Josephine looking at him. "He might be if he ever ran a comb through that frazzled hair," she said.

"Maybe you could help him. You know, clean him up a bit. Throw out those ridiculous Bert and Ernie slippers."

"His grandkids gave them to him," she mumbled, taking another a sip of water.

"Huh?"

She slammed her water down on the table and some sloshed out onto the peach tablecloth. "I said his grandkids gave those to him for a present. That's why he wears them. I shouldn't know this, but I do because he yaps in my ear every chance he gets."

"*Aw.* That's so sweet. He's a loving grandfather. Do his grandkids come and visit him in here?"

"Yes."

"Have you met them?"

She let out a loud breath. "Yes, he did introduce me. Of course. He's got so many, though. Can't hardly keep track of all of them."

I grinned at her. "They love their grandpa, don't they?"

"It appears they do."

"Why don't you give him a chance?"

"Like I said, I don't need to have to take care of no man." She shook her head. "No sir. Don't need to be runnin' a comb through that frazzled hair."

"He doesn't need you to take care of him. He gets plenty of good care in here." I stared at her. "You just can't believe that someone might actually like you for you."

Her eyes met mine. "Ditto, little girl."

Make a choice.
Find my voice.
Not sure I can.
I need a new plan.

—Kids from Alcatraz

THE MOST AMAZING THING happened. And that thing is called the weather dropped below ninety degrees. I wasn't sure if it would last, but it was wonderful. And I was also grateful that the drop in temperature coincided with another riding lesson. There was something especially uncomfortable about sitting on a big hot horse in one hundred degree weather—kind of like how getting branded must be uncomfortable for cows.

"The horse show is next month already," Bill said. "You ready to try the jump?"

"No."

"Aven, do you even want to do this show?" He took

off his cowboy hat and ran a hand through his gray hair. Then he put his hat back on. "Because you know you don't have to."

I stared down at Bill. Did I want to do the show? When I'd first had the idea to start horseback riding, I'd felt so confident, so sure I could tackle anything. And at the beginning of the school year, nothing could have stopped me from doing that jump. Now the fear I felt about it overwhelmed me.

High school was stealing everything away from me—my courage, my confidence, and my determination. And I'd only barely started. Four more years of this would kill me. I finally shrugged. "I don't know."

Bill hung his head for a moment. "Tell you what. We'll hold off on the jump. How about we work on trotting for today?"

I cringed. I didn't want to do that either. Trotting made me bounce all over the place and I felt like I was going to bounce right off Chili. Plus, it hurt my butt and I was always sore the next day. Not to mention that my ankle was still tender, making it difficult to use my feet to pull on the reins.

Bill gave up, and we walked around a little and practiced some simple voice commands. Instead of feeling happy, though, that Bill had eased up on pushing me, I felt worse. Because I knew he was giving up on me.

After my lesson, I checked on Spaghetti. I expected him to be a bit more energetic with the drop in temperature, but he was as lethargic as ever. "What is going on with you?" I said to him as I nuzzled his soft fur. I offered him a piece of broccoli, which was a special treat for him. Last spring, he'd have eaten it right up. But now he wouldn't even glance at it. I held the broccoli with my toes and tapped it gently on his mouth, but he didn't acknowledge it. I gave up and decided to go home.

When I walked into the apartment, both of my parents were sitting at the kitchen table. They stopped talking when they saw me.

"What's up?" I asked.

"How was your riding lesson?" Dad said.

"It was good," I lied. I didn't have the heart to tell them I would never be ready for the horse show.

"That's great," Mom said, squeezing her hands together.

I looked from Mom to Dad. It was odd for them to both be in the apartment this early in the day. "What's going on?"

"We got something for you," Mom said.

I tilted my head a little. "Okay. Why do you seem so nervous?"

Mom picked up a box from the table. "It's this."

I walked to her and read the box in her hands. "Find My Family," I said. "What is it?"

"It's a DNA testing kit," Dad said.

"What for?"

"For you," they both said together.

Mom set the box back down on the table. "It's for you to send in."

"Why?"

They exchanged glances. "You might be able to find your father or someone in your father's family with it," Dad said.

I stood there staring at them, not knowing what to say. I wasn't sure how I felt about this. I wasn't kidding when I told Zion's family I didn't like surprises. And this was a big one. I felt completely unprepared.

"It's just that," Mom said, "ever since you found out Josephine is your grandmother and that your birth mother died, you keep bringing up your birth father. We understand if you're curious about who he is, so we thought this might help you find that out."

I stared down at the box like it was a scorpion sitting on our kitchen table, its venom-filled tail pointed directly at me. But it was just a box. "I'm mostly joking when I say that stuff."

"Maybe sometimes you are," Mom said. "But sometimes you're not. There must be a reason why you keep mentioning him to us and to Josephine."

"All you have to do is spit in a tube, Sheebs, and send it in," Dad said. "Simple as that."

Simple as that.

"Then they'll contact you if you have a DNA connection to anyone in the database," Mom added.

I kept staring at the box—just a harmless box. How could a box feel so scary? Even if I took it, that didn't mean I had to use it. I didn't have to make this huge life-changing choice right here in the middle of the kitchen at this very moment.

Mom and Dad were staring at me, so I picked it up between my chin and shoulder and carried it to my room. I set it on my desk, then sat down and stared at it some more. "Find My Family," I said to myself.

But did I want to? What if he was a bad person? Like, what if he was an actual real-life meanie? What if he was a big bully like Joshua? What if he was a snob like Janessa? I wasn't sure I could handle that. What if finding him was another great big disappointment in my life right now?

Or worse, what if I was a disappointment to him?

Leave me alone
So I can wallow.
Go away.
Please don't follow.

—We Are Librarians

"HEY," LANDO SAID, WALKING UP
behind me at my locker. "You having trouble with that?"

I dropped the lock from my toes with frustration.
"Always," I said. "I am always having trouble with that."

"What's your code?" Lando asked.

I looked around. "I can't tell you that out loud." Since
my locker had nothing in it besides textbooks and garbage, literally, I was a lot more concerned about what
someone might put *in* my locker when I wasn't looking
than what they might take out.

Lando leaned in close and put his ear to my mouth.
"Whisper it to me."

I suddenly couldn't remember my code as I stood

there frozen, breathing in Lando's ear. "Uh . . . three, sixteen, eleven," I said.

He bent down and unlocked my locker for me. "What do you need?" he asked.

What did I need? What classes did I have this afternoon? I tried to take all my books for my morning classes and all my books for my afternoon classes at the same time so I'd only have to visit my locker twice per day.

Lando looked up at me, his eyes as bright as his smile. "Algebra, Bio, and English," I told him.

I was so incredibly glad I'd recently cleaned the rotting peanut butter and jelly sandwich out of my locker as he hunted for my books. "Do you want to keep these?" he asked as he opened my shoulder bag.

"No, those can go back."

He exchanged my books then slammed my locker shut and relocked it. He stood up and faced me. "You have algebra right now?"

"Yeah."

"You want to walk together?"

I took a step back. "Why?"

Lando frowned. "Geez, Aven, why you always asking me why? Why I want to dance with you. Why I want to walk with you."

"Well . . ." I slipped my foot in and out of my flip-flop. "Why do you?"

"You think I have some ulterior motive?"

I looked down at my green flip-flop and shook my head. "I don't know." I glanced up at him. "Do you?"

"Did it ever occur to you that I like hanging out with you?"

I was about to ask why, but stopped myself. "You have a lot of other friends to hang out with."

Lando's head shot back, and I realized how that had sounded, but that wasn't how I'd meant it. Why would Lando want to hang out with me when he could hang out with kids who were cooler than me?

"Harsh, Aven. If you want me to leave you alone—"

"I think that would be best. For everybody."

Lando stared at me for a moment, and I looked back down at my flip-flops. I didn't want him to see the tears forming in my eyes as he turned around and walked away.

*I'm losing myself
My own voice I can't hear.
Put my feelings on the shelf.
Except anger and fear.*

—Kids from Alcatraz

CONNOR AND I SAT IN THE
rocking chairs on the front porch of the soda shop
together eating ice cream.

"You're so quiet today," he said. "I could have sat at
home by myself not talking to anyone. Again."

"Sorry," I said.

"What's wrong now?"

Everything. Everything was wrong. "I don't know," I
said, which was sort of true. I was confused—confused
about whether I wanted to find my birth father, confused about whether I wanted to ride in the horse show
anymore, confused about Lando.

Lando was Zion's brother, so we should be friends,

right? Why had things gotten so weird with him? Why did he ask me to dance? Why did he want to walk with me to class? Was he feeling sorry for me? That was the absolute worst thing I could think of—that he felt sorry for me and was trying to hang out with me out of pity. And it was made worse by the fact that every time I thought about him, my heart sped up a little bit, and my feet shook a little bit, and my mouth went a little bit dry.

I couldn't *like* Lando. Not *like* him, like him. I was sure lots of girls liked Lando. I would be setting myself up for major disappointment. If only I could shut it off. Josephine was so unhelpful.

Connor barked, startling me out of my thoughts. "So what's up with you and Lando?" he asked, as though he had been able to hear the ramblings in my head.

I turned to him. "Why are you asking me about him?"

He shrugged. "Zion told me you all went to homecoming together and that you freaked out and busted up your ankle when Lando asked you to dance with him."

I scowled. "Geez, does everyone have to know everything?"

"I think if you had it your way, no one would know anything."

"What's that supposed to mean?"

"Just that you've been awfully secretive about stuff lately."

"What stuff?"

"How should I know? You're all secretive about it."

"Maybe I don't want people in my business," I said. "Sometimes I wish everyone would leave me alone."

"Including me." Connor blinked his eyes and clucked his tongue as he frowned down at his ice cream.

"Well, how am I supposed to be a hermit when everyone's always bugging me?"

Connor got up and threw his ice cream in the trash. "You better be careful, Aven, or you might get your wish." He walked down the steps, and I watched as he walked across the dirt to the petting zoo. He sat down in the dirt with Spaghetti.

The door of the soda shop opened and Henry walked outside. "Everything okay?" he asked. "You two don't seem very happy."

"I don't feel very happy," I said. "I feel all messed up."

"Messed up, huh?" Henry sat down in a rocking chair. He smiled at me, and I was glad he was having a good day.

"I hate high school," I told him.

"Is it all that bad?"

"It's the worst."

Henry and I sat there quietly. At one point Connor glanced over at me and gave me a dirty look. Henry chuckled. "So what are you two fighting about?"

"I don't know. I told him I wanted everyone to leave me alone so I could proceed with my plans to become a hermit and he got all offended."

"A hermit, huh?" Henry said. "How are you going to ride in the horse show if you're a hermit?"

"I won't. I won't ride in the horse show. I won't go to school. I won't have to deal with boys making fun of me. I won't have to deal with questions about my birth father. I won't have to deal with fights with my friends and cranky grandmothers." I took a deep breath. "Sounds like heaven."

"*Hm*," Henry said. "Sounds like you're being a big chicken."

I glared at him. "I am not."

"Sounds like you want to hide from life instead of facing it head on." Henry shook his head. "I guess I don't know you as well as I thought I did."

"Half the time you don't know who I am at all."

Henry looked sadly across at the petting zoo.

"I'm sorry," I said, shaking my head. "I shouldn't

have said that. I don't know what's wrong with me. High school is making me crazy."

"I never thought you'd let something as silly as high school beat you."

I bit down on my lip. "When I finished last year, I felt like . . . like I could face anything. And then Connor moved away, and this boy . . ."

Henry's eyes cut to me. "This boy, what?"

"He humiliated me. And he keeps humiliating me. And I keep getting farther and farther away from myself, like I'm up in a plane and I'm trying to find myself down on earth, but I'm just a little speck I can't even see, and I'm like, 'Hey, Aven! It's me, Aven!' But I'm a tiny speck, so I don't know if I can see myself."

Henry looked incredibly confused, which made sense, since what I said made *no* sense at all. "I'm not sure about anything anymore," I told him. "I'm not sure if someone really likes me or if he's, I don't know, making fun of me, I guess. I don't think he would, but I feel like I can't trust anyone anymore."

Henry nodded. "You going to let one mean boy have this much power over you?" He looked back at the petting zoo. "You going to let him ruin your friendships? You going to let him ruin what should be the best years of your life?"

"Whoever said high school is the best years of your life was probably homeschooled." I watched Connor. He glanced up at me then quickly turned his attention back to Spaghetti. I smiled. "How'd you get so wise anyway, Henry?"

"I'm old," he declared. "Lots of time to get lots of wisdom. And I was bullied, too, you know. There were always bullies in the orphanages."

"Were there?"

"Oh, yeah. And I didn't have a family to help me through it. But I did have friends—good friends in the orphanages. We helped each other. I don't know what I'd have done without them. But I know I wouldn't have let silly arguments ruin our friendships."

"I'm sorry you didn't have family to help you through your hard times," I said. "I guess I'm lucky in some ways."

Henry grunted. "You're lucky in lots of ways. And friends can be like family. There're all different kinds of families." Henry pointed at Connor. "Friends can be like family."

I smiled at Henry. Then I got up and made my way to the petting zoo. I sat down next to Connor and Spaghetti on the ground. Connor didn't look at me as he kept rubbing his fur. He played music on his phone for Spaghetti.

"You really think he likes Llama Parade?" I asked Connor.

"It's only his favorite band. Of course."

"Of course. They're one of my favorite bands, too."

"He seems awfully tired still," Connor said.

"Yeah." I slipped my foot out of my flip-flop and ran it along Spaghetti's soft fur. "He never has any energy anymore."

"He's skinny. I can feel his ribs poking through."

"He doesn't eat much. He won't even eat special treats like broccoli or potatoes."

"I'm worried about him."

I nodded. "I am, too."

A goat ran across the petting zoo and head-butted another goat. The unsuspecting goat fell over on his side, completely stiff, his legs jutting out all funny. Connor and I giggled.

"I'm sorry," I said. "I've been a huge jerk. And the worst part is, I keep being a huge jerk."

Connor shrugged. "Why do you keep being a jerk?"

I shook my head. "I wish we could go back to the way things were."

"I wish that, too, Aven. But we can't control everything." He slowly ran his fingers through Spaghetti's fur, and I saw how calm Connor was. He wasn't ticcing at all.

"Spaghetti would have made a good therapy llama," I said.

Connor smiled. "Maybe he could still be one."

How could Spaghetti be a therapy llama when he couldn't eat? Could barely walk? I'd hardly seen him on his feet lately.

"I think it's too late for him," I said.

When it's almost over
Promise me you'll be there.
When it's almost over
Promise me you'll care.

—Llama Parade

I FOUND THE COURAGE TO SPEAK

to Lando the following week at school. "Hi."

He looked around. "You talking to me?"

I nodded. "Yes."

"Oh," he said. "Because I thought it was best if I left you alone. So I'm going to do that now."

My heart felt like a stake was in it as I watched Lando walk away. I wanted him to leave me alone. But I also completely and totally didn't want him to leave me alone. My brain had never felt so dysfunctional, and normally it was pretty high functioning.

I trudged to the cafeteria and sat down with Zion at our usual table. "Why you being so mean to my brother, huh?" he said the moment my butt touched the seat.

I slumped in my chair. I didn't want to eat anything. "Why are you asking me that?"

"Because he said that you totally dissed him."

"He told you that?"

"Yeah." Zion crossed his arms. I found his little defensive act on behalf of Lando really sweet.

"I don't understand you guys," I said. "One minute you're defending each other and the next you're about to beat each other up. Then you're defending each other again."

"We're brothers."

"Well, I guess I don't get brothers. And I definitely don't get why Lando cares about how I treat him." I glanced over at Lando's table. "Look at all the friends he has."

"So *you* can't be his friend?"

"Of course I can be his friend."

"Then what's the big deal?"

"Maybe I don't want to be his friend!"

"Why? Do you hate him?"

I let my head fall onto the lunch table with a satisfying *thwap*. "I don't hate him at all," I mumbled. "I completely the opposite of hate him."

I finally looked up at Zion, my forehead throbbing. He had his mouth open in a small circle the size of a Cheerio.

"Please don't tell anybody," I said. "Especially not him."

"He thinks you don't like him at all."

"Good," I said. "It's better that way."

"I don't think so. I think you're torturing yourself for no reason. It's better to be friends than nothing at all."

I squinted at him. "Have you called Trilby since homecoming?"

Zion's eyes shot down to his sandwich. "No."

"Why not? Didn't you guys have a nice time together?"

"I guess."

"Why don't you call her? I think she likes you."

Zion shook his head. "There's no way she could like me."

"Then why did she agree to go to homecoming with you?"

"You heard her. Because she always thought she'd never get to go to dances, being a homeschooler and all."

"So . . . you think she was using you? You're starting to sound like my grandma."

"Josephine?"

"Yeah. You sound like an old lady."

"No. I sound like you, which means you're the one who sounds like an old lady."

I saw Henry sitting in a rocking chair as I walked through Stagecoach Pass after school that day. I walked up the steps. "Hey, Henry."

He sat there staring, his mouth hung open, completely still. "Henry?"

He didn't move. I nudged him with my foot. "Henry?"

He slowly turned his head to me. "*Hm*?"

"Are you okay?" I sat down in a rocking chair next to him.

"*Hm*?" he said again then stared off at nothing.

"Henry?" I said more sharply this time.

He looked at me again. "Oh, hi," he said slowly.

"Hi. Do you know who I am?"

"Aven Cavanaugh."

"No, I'm Aven Green. I'm going to go get my dad."

As I walked down the steps, I heard Henry say, "But you don't have a dad."

Dad and I helped Henry upstairs to his apartment. Henry was so confused, I wasn't sure he knew who Dad was.

While Dad helped Henry get into bed, I walked around the tiny apartment, like something in there might offer a clue about Henry's past. But it was bare—no pictures, no decorations, no personal touches. Just the minimum amount of furniture a person needed to live. There should have been photographs of friends and family and souvenirs he'd collected on vacations and gifts he'd been given by people who loved him. The thought of him growing up in the orphanages made my chest hurt. And the thought of him living here in this sparse apartment all these years broke my heart.

Henry didn't even have a TV. There was only a small shelf of books. I scanned over the titles, but they were mostly old touristy type books about Arizona. I imagined some of them had come from the souvenir shop who knows how long ago. It was like a hotel room Henry had only planned on staying in a short time.

I sat down on Henry's small worn sofa and waited for Dad. He came out of Henry's room and sat next to me. He sighed as he rubbed his eyes and forehead.

"Is he going to be okay?" I asked.

"I don't know. He seems to be getting worse all the time."

"Some days are good."

"Yeah, but those are getting fewer and farther

between." Dad put an arm around me and squeezed. "I don't want you to worry about it, Sheebs. You have enough to worry about right now."

But I *was* worried about Henry. And I was worried he would die without ever knowing where he had come from and whether he had any family out there searching for him.

*Now is the time
When it will all collide.
Did you think it wouldn't?
Did you think you could hide?*

—Screaming Ferret

"HOW MUCH LONGER CAN HE KEEP working?" Zion asked as we sat on a bench at school the next morning.

"I don't know," I said. "We keep him there because it gives him a purpose, something to do. I've read that once old people stop working, they die more quickly."

"Do you think he's going to die?"

"I hope not," I said. "But I don't think he can keep going on like this much longer."

"Where's he going to go?"

"Golden Sunset has an assisted living section. Anyway, that's the plan."

"Does he know that?"

"Oh, yeah. But he said he doesn't want to go until he can no longer lift the ice cream scoop." I thought about him—the day he struggled to scoop the ice cream and dropped it all over the floor. It felt like maybe that day had come.

Joshua walked by with some friends. He blew me a kiss. I was so completely sick of this. "Keep your diseases to yourself," I said to him.

He detoured and walked in our direction with his friends. They stopped in front of us. "I'm the one who's diseased?" he said.

"You don't seem to know the difference between a disease and genetics," I told him. "Maybe you should grow a brain so you can understand."

"And maybe you should grow some arms so you can be less freakish."

I stared at him as his friends snickered around him. I decided to ask him a question, a question that had been forming in my mind since the day this all started. I didn't ask it to be mean, or to hurt him, or to embarrass him in any way. I asked because I truly wanted to know the answer. Because I *had* to know the answer. Because there had to be a reason for all of this. "Why are you such a bad person?"

His smile fell for a moment. For once he didn't

seem to have anything to say. His mouth opened like he would make his retort. Then closed. Then it opened again. But before Joshua could speak, Lando was there next to him. Joshua turned to him.

"Get away from them," Lando said, getting up in Joshua's face. Instantly people were crowding around, sensing a fight about to start. High schoolers were worse than ancient Romans.

Joshua didn't back down, though. He was surrounded by his friends and had to save face, though he seemed nervous. "Sorry," he said. "I didn't mean to offend your fat brother and his freaky girlfriend."

Lando clenched his jaw. "What did you just say?" he asked through gritted teeth.

Joshua just stood there, a horrible smirk on his face. "You know what I said."

Then we heard an adult voice shout, "What's going on here?" Instantly kids started dispersing and Lando backed away from Joshua, who gave us all one last slimy smirk before walking away.

A teacher walked up to us and asked, "Everything okay over here?"

Lando adjusted his backpack over his shoulder, glanced down at Zion and me. "It's fine," he mumbled then walked off.

* * *

I sat on my bed trying to focus on my English home-work. Every now and then I'd glance at the Find My Family box sitting on my desk, like it might slink over and attack me at any moment if I didn't keep an eye on it. My phone buzzed on the floor and I swung my legs around. I hated that every time I saw my cracked screen it reminded me of that horrible day. It was Zion, so I hit the answer and speaker buttons with my toes.

"Hey."

"Hi," he said tentatively.

"Is everything okay?" I asked.

"Um, no. Not really."

"What's wrong?"

"My parents are all upset because Lando quit the football team today."

I stood up from the bed. "What? Why?"

"He and Joshua started yelling at each other out on the field, and when the coach tried to intervene, Lando said he couldn't be on the same team as Joshua and quit. Just threw his helmet down and walked off the field."

I shook my head as I sat back down. "No. No, he can't do that. He loves football. Why would he do that?"

Zion was quiet for a while before finally saying, "Aven, I have to tell you something."

"What?"

"I told Lando about what happened at the mall."

I jumped back up. Lando knew about my Great Humiliation? No, no, no, no. "What? When?"

Zion stayed quiet.

"When?" I demanded again.

"Right before practice."

Now I did cry. "I trusted you. You said you wouldn't tell anyone. Why did you tell him?"

"Because he kept asking me stuff," Zion defended himself. "Like why you didn't like him. And I told him it wasn't that you don't like him."

"You told him I like him?" I shrieked.

"I told him that I think you're scared after what Joshua did to you. I think you're scared of getting embarrassed again."

Tears slid down my cheeks. "Well, it's too late because I could never be more embarrassed than I am now." I hit the end call button.

I DIDN'T GO FIND ZION THE NEXT
day at lunch. I was so angry with him for telling Lando
about my Great Humiliation. It made it worse—like I
was reliving the whole thing. The thought that it had
anything at all to do with Lando quitting football made
it so much worse.

I went to the library during lunch that day. I sat at
a table alone and wished Connor were there with me. I
felt more alone than I had on that day last year when I'd
first met him. I looked around but no one was in there
but the librarian.

I wanted to scream when I saw Joshua on my way
to the bus that afternoon. He should have been the one

off the football team. Not Lando. Instead of screaming, I ran away when I saw him. Josephine was right. Zion was right. Henry was right. I was a big chicken. I'd become scared of everything.

After the bus dropped me off, I walked through Stagecoach Pass. The crowds were picking up, and a handful of people walked the streets. I couldn't deal with their stares today. I ran up the steps of the soda shop to see how Henry was doing.

Henry wasn't behind the counter, though. "Henry?" I called to the back. But he didn't come out. I walked around to the back of the counter.

And there was Henry, lying on the floor, face down. I rushed to him and knelt down. "Henry!" I cried, but he didn't move. I jumped up and looked at the phone on the wall of the soda shop—it was one of those old-fashioned kinds. I had no idea how to use it, nor did I think I would be capable of doing so even if I did know how.

I dropped my bag to the floor and struggled to get the strap off from around my neck as it caught in my hair. I pulled and pulled, tears blurring my vision. I finally managed to get it off, kicked my flip-flops off, and threw myself down on my butt. I started digging around in my bag with my feet. I couldn't find my phone. This was taking too long. I couldn't find my stupid phone with my stupid feet. I turned the bag over and shook it with my feet to empty it. Henry might die because I couldn't get to my phone fast enough.

I finally found my phone, but my stupid fat toe was shaking as I tried to dial, and I kept hitting the wrong buttons. "Stupid," I muttered through clenched teeth, tears falling onto the screen. "Stupid . . . stupid . . . stupid no arms!" I cried as I jumped back up to my feet. I ran to the doors and slammed through them with my side. "I need help!"

Mom and Dad sat in the maroon chairs of the hospital waiting room while I paced across the gray linoleum floor. "Honey," Mom said, "why don't you sit down?"

But I couldn't sit down. I felt like I could run and run for miles and still not relieve the tension in my body.

Dad stood up and put a hand to my back. "It's okay, Aven." He wrapped his arm around me and squeezed me tightly to his chest.

"Where is he?" a frantic voice called. I rubbed my eyes against Dad's shirt then looked up at Josephine. "Where's Henry?"

"He's getting an MRI right now," Dad said as he ran a hand down my hair. "They think it was a stroke."

Josephine's hands shot to her mouth. "Oh, no."

"It's a good thing Aven found him when she did," Dad said. "The doctor said every second counts." Dad smiled down at me. "He might not even be alive right now if it weren't for her."

Dad's words should have made me feel good, but nothing could cut through my worry. Not just my worry that Henry would die, but my fear that he would die without ever having known where he really came from. I didn't know why it had become so important to me that he know. Maybe it was because I knew what it felt like to wonder where you'd come from and why your parents had given you away. To wonder if they regretted doing so. To wonder if they'd ever loved you at all. To wonder if *he* even knew I existed.

My mind wandered to the Find My Family box still sitting on my desk just as the doctor walked into the waiting room. Mom shot up from her seat. "How is he?" she asked.

The doctor smiled warmly at us. "He's doing well," she said. "He did have a minor stroke, but we already had him on IV blood thinners to dissolve the clot in anticipation of that finding. He also has a fairly large bump on his head from where he must have hit it on the floor, so we're keeping a close eye on that as well."

"What about brain damage?" Josephine asked.

"It's a little early to tell," the doctor said. "We'll know more when he wakes up, when we see whether he's talking and how much he understands. But like I said, it was a minor stroke. The clot was fairly small, so we have high hopes." She looked down at me. "You're the one who found him?"

I nodded. "I always visit him after school." I glanced up at Mom and Dad. "And not just for ice cream."

Mom and Dad both smiled and wrapped their arms around me as the doctor said, "If more elderly had people regularly checking in on them, a lot more people could be saved." She squeezed my shoulder. "Good job."

"Can we see him?" Josephine asked.

"We're still running more tests, so I'd say probably not until tomorrow at the soonest," the doctor said. "He's not conscious anyway, but I'll make sure to have someone call you if he wakes up."

It was getting late and we decided there was nothing we could do to help Henry by sitting in the waiting room, so we headed home. The four of us sat down at a table in the steakhouse for a late dinner. "I've known Henry a long time," Josephine said, picking at her side salad (a new addition to the menu). "Longer than anyone. He's strong. He's going to pull through this."

"There you all are," Denise said, walking up to our table. "How's Henry? We're all so worried about him."

"Too soon to tell," Mom said. "But it was a minor stroke. The doctors are hopeful he'll recover."

"That's good," Denise said, wringing her hands. She didn't look relieved at all. She kept glancing at me, then at our food, then at me. "I really hate to drop this on you right now," she finally said. "But I'm sure you'd want to know."

If this was more bad news, I didn't think I could take it. And why was she looking at *me*?

"It's Spaghetti."

Everyone's eyes shot to me as my stomach dropped out and my throat went completely dry. "I'm so sorry, Aven," Denise said, her voice cracking, her eyes instantly filling. "I found him this evening after all the chaos." She sniffled and wiped at her cheek. "He's gone."

I think there comes a point when your sadness gets too great that you can no longer feel anything at all. You just become numb. Because in that moment, I couldn't possibly grieve for Henry and Spaghetti and my friendship with Zion and everything else going wrong in my life at the same time. I think I'd finally run out of tears. And I didn't even know that was possible.

31

I can't go on.
I don't have the will.
I can't make it
Up this giant hill.

—Kids from Alcatraz

I FELT LIKE I WAS IN A CONSTANT DAZE
over the next week, so overwhelmed with everything.
There was no one for me to talk to, even if I could find
words to say. The people I wanted to talk to were gone,
and the people who wanted to talk to me I pushed away.
The only thing I could do was write down how I felt.

My mom has told me that God never gives us
more than we can handle, which is apparently why
I was born without arms—because dude thought I
could handle it. But I think I'm pretty much maxed
out at the moment. I can't handle one more thing.
I could probably come up with about a thousand

hard things about my life right now, but I'll only give you twenty:

1.   Three thousand kids. And I haven't made friends with even one percent of them. Not even with one percent of one percent of them, which is only like a third of a person. That's how bad things are. At least I'm still good at math.

2.   My math skills aren't exactly reeling in the friends.

3.   Stupid feelings. I wish I didn't have them. Androids have the good life.

4.   My only career choices at the moment are hermit, llama, and android.

5.   I still have to go to school every day.

6.   I saw an article online about "trust issues," and I'm pretty sure I have them.

7.   I think Fathead is dead. Aven's Tarantula Rehabilitation Center is a massive failure.

8. I'm going to disappoint everyone when I don't ride in the horse show.

9. I miss smoothies, and I miss hanging out with Trilby in the smoothie shop.

10. Keeping secrets is hard. I've become a liar.

11. I'm being bullied at school. And I don't know what to do about it.

12. I always thought I was strong, but it only took one mean person to bring me down. I'm weak.

13. I feel like my best friend is drifting away from me. Or replacing me.

14. I have a huge choice to make. And I don't think I have the will to make it. I wish someone else could make it for me.

15. Henry is in the hospital fighting for his life. If he dies, his untold history dies with him.

16. Everyone keeps telling me I'm a chicken.

17. I *am* a chicken.

18. I like someone. I *like* him, like him. And I wish I didn't.

19. The person I like is suffering because of me.

20. And the worst thing of all, the thing that has pushed me to my absolute maximum capacity for sadness, is that I now have a funeral to plan.

If you only knew.
Don't be like me.
Be like you.

—Kids from Alcatraz

I STARED OUT THE WINDOW OF THE
bus, hoping no one had any comments for me today.
I just felt . . . sad. I glanced at the kids getting on in
time to see Lando walk up the bus steps. I watched as
he meandered down the aisle, scanning the seats. I
hunched down.

He stopped when he got to my row. "Can I sit with
you?"

I nodded.

Lando sat down next to me and shoved his backpack underneath the seat in front of us with his feet.
We sat quietly like that for the next twenty minutes as
the bus got less and less rowdy and more and more kids

got off. I wondered if he was ever going to say something because I knew I wouldn't speak first.

I stared out the dingy window, which made everything outside look sad and gross. I felt a sting on my leg. I gawked down at the tiny red spot forming on my pale thigh. I glared at Lando. "Did you . . . flick me?"

He seemed offended at my accusation. "It was a total accident."

I squinted at him. "You *accidentally* flicked my leg?"

"Total accident."

"You are such a liar," I said, laughing a little.

"I'm not sorry about it, either."

I laughed more. "That's nice."

He shrugged. "I don't do anything for no reason."

I swallowed. "Like quitting football?"

"Like I said, I don't do anything for no reason." We sat quietly until he finally said. "Are you okay, Aven?"

I shook my head. "I don't know."

"I'm really sorry about Spaghetti. Zion told me you emailed him about the memorial. He said it was a very formal email."

"I don't have a lot to say to him right now."

"He feels awful about everything. I hate to see you both so upset. You're best friends."

"Which is why I trusted him with very sensitive information."

"You can still trust him. He would never do anything to deliberately hurt you. Will you please talk to him? Please?"

The bus halted, and I saw we were at my stop. I stared out the grimy window at the Stagecoach Pass parking lot. "Okay," I whispered.

Lando grabbed my bag strap and placed it around my neck. "So do you think your parents will give me a ride home?" he asked sheepishly.

"You didn't think this through, did you?"

Lando smiled. "I totally did."

We walked quietly through the entrance of Stagecoach Pass, glancing at each other every now and then.

Lando swung his backpack around. "I have something for you." He unzipped it and pulled out a stack of papers. He opened my bag and slipped them inside.

"What is it?" I asked.

"You'll see. Just read it when you get home."

"Okay."

We kept walking, and Lando kicked at a rock in the middle of Main Street. It bounced off a rusty metal trashcan and made a loud *clang*. "So it's Halloween next week," he said.

"Yeah, so?"

"So, I'm dressing up."

"You are not."

"I am, too. I already have a costume."

"You are not wearing your Captain America costume to school. No one dresses up anymore. Everyone thinks you're a huge dweeb if you dress up."

Lando stopped, serious now. He adjusted his backpack over his shoulder. "Do I look like I care about what anyone else does or thinks, Aven?"

I glanced at him and then moved my eyes to the ground, ashamed of what I had said. "No. No, I don't think you do."

"When are you going to realize that what other people think doesn't matter?"

I bit my lip. "Sorry," I whispered.

"Don't be sorry."

I opened my mouth to say sorry again but stopped myself. I watched my dusty feet as we continued making our way along the dirt road, Lando walking quietly next me. "I wish I could be more like you," I said.

Lando stopped, and I stopped and looked up at him. He stood there for what felt like the longest time, staring at me, studying me, like he was trying to figure something out. Figure me out. Or maybe he already had. Finally he said, "And I wish you could be more like you."

As soon as Dad left to take Lando home, I went to my room and pulled out the stack of papers Lando had shoved in my bag. I sat down on the floor and stared at the stack, slowly sorting through the pages with my toes.

They were drawings of . . . me.

Me with a long green cape and mask, blazing red hair swirling in every direction around my masked face.

Me in my Armless Master costume, defending my friends from snarling bullies, wildly whirling nunchuks held in my toes.

Me in my purple dress with bright purple streaks in my red hair, playing a guitar with my feet, my mouth open with musical notes flowing from it.

Me riding a flying llamacorn across a cloudless desert sky.

Me . . . as I had always wished to be.

You've pushed me down.
I may be low.
But you're stuck where you are.
And I have room to grow.

—The Square Pegs

THE NEXT DAY, I FOUND COACH

Devin's office and kicked gently on the door.

"Come in," he called from inside.

I gripped the handle between my chin and shoulder and opened the door. His eyes widened when he saw me. "Hello," he said. "Can I help you with something?"

I cleared my throat and wiggled to adjust my shoulder bag. "Um, yes. My name is Aven Green."

"You're a friend of Lando's brother, aren't you?"

I nodded.

"I see you two watching practice sometimes."

I bit my lip. "Yeah, I guess we kind of stand out."

He smiled. "That's not what I meant. Not many

people sit out there watching in the heat." He motioned toward a seat in the corner of the small room. "Would you like to sit down?"

My legs felt shaky as I took a deep breath. "I'm here about Lando."

Coach Devin leaned forward on his elbows and steepled his fingers over the desk. "Yeah, I'm really disappointed he quit the team. He's a good player."

"He quit because of Joshua Baker."

He put his hands down. "Yes, he told me that."

"But he didn't tell you why."

"It really doesn't matter. We're always going to butt heads with people. It's good to learn how to work with people you have disagreements with."

I studied the thin blue, worn carpet of the office floor. "This is so much more than a disagreement," I said. I looked up at the coach. "Doesn't this school have a strict anti-bullying policy?"

The coach nodded. "Of course. But I can't see anyone bullying Lando. He seems fairly popular."

"It's not Lando who's being bullied. It's Zion and me."

Coach Devin furrowed his brow. "Do you want to tell me what's been going on?"

"I do," I said, my voice cracking. I swallowed and cleared my throat. "I want to tell you everything."

It's time to say goodbye.
I'll carry you with me forever.
It's time for me to cry.
But our bond will never sever.

—Llama Parade

I SAT IN MY ROOM ON MY BED, staring at the box of ashes on my side table. Then I looked over at the Find My Family box on my desk. Too many boxes. Too many feelings.

I heard a knock and walked out to the living room. Mom opened the door, and Connor and his mom came in. "Hey," Connor said to me, giving me a sad smile.

"Hey," I said. "Hi, Mrs. Bradley."

She gave me a sad smile and a hug. "Hi, Aven. I'm so sorry."

I nodded into her chest. "It's okay," I said.

The door was still open as Zion and Lando walked in with their parents. I pulled away from Mrs. Bradley.

"Thank you for coming," I said. Zion stared down at the floor. I stepped a little closer to him. "Thank you for coming." He finally looked up at me, his head still low, his eyebrows raised. I smiled a little. He smiled back a little. We were a little okay.

Mrs. Hill gave me a hug and squeezed me so tight I could barely breathe while Zion and Connor did a sad little fist bump.

Connor, Zion, and I sat on the couch while the grown-ups chatted about boring stuff—the kind of stuff you talk about to pass time. I glanced at Lando and his eyes caught mine. I got up and stood in a corner of the room with him. "Hi," I said.

"Hi."

"Thanks for coming."

"Of course. I know he was important to you."

I nodded and bit my lip and forbade myself to cry again. I think I'd shed more tears since starting high school than I had in all fourteen years of my life before it.

"Joshua's been suspended," Lando said.

I did my best to act surprised. "Really?"

Lando studied my face. "Yes. And that means he can't play football."

I cleared my throat. "Really? Does that mean . . ."

Lando tilted his head down at me. "That I'm going to play again?"

I nodded.

His face lit up with his bright smile. "Yeah, Coach asked me to come back."

"That's so great." I kicked at the nearby baseboard, studied the patterns in the stuccoed wall. I felt awkward standing there with him, not sure what else to say, so I turned to go sit back down with Connor and Zion.

"Hey, Aven," Lando said. I turned around. "Thank you."

"For what?"

"For sticking up for me."

I blushed. I didn't think the coach would tell Lando about me—that I had gone to him and told him everything that had happened, including the Great Humiliation and all things since. It had been a hard choice but one that was necessary to set things right. "I didn't think he would tell you."

Lando smiled. "He didn't."

I wanted to say something about his beautiful drawings, about what they meant to me, how they made me feel. But I struggled to find the right words. "Your drawings," I started to say. Lando's eyes widened and he looked at me expectantly, but then Josephine walked in . . . with Milford.

The whole room went quiet. "Hi, Josephine," Mom said. "We're so glad to see you." They gave each other a polite hug. "Who's this handsome gentleman?"

"It's Milford," I said, not able to keep from smiling.

"Hi, Aven," he said shyly and hugged me. Funerals sure were huggy things.

"Nice to meet you, Milford," Dad said while I grinned slyly at Josephine, who rolled her eyes at me.

"Is he your date?" I whispered to her.

She huffed. "One does not bring a date to a funeral."

"Then what is it?"

"It's a sociable outing together."

After Denise and Trilby and her parents and a few other workers showed up, we all made our way, one long procession, up the hill behind Stagecoach Pass. I stood next to my giant saguaro, and I realized it had been one year since I'd sat here and compared my insignificant troubles to all the monumental events that had taken place in the last couple of centuries during the life of this one cactus. As insignificant as I tried to make my worries feel, they were still important to me. And today was the same. The difference, though, was that I was alone then. Today I was surrounded by people who cared about me.

I steadied my breathing and began to speak. "Spaghetti was the best llama ever. He was a great friend.

An attentive listener. He never rambled on and on about himself. He never judged." My voice cracked a little.

I took a deep breath. "He knew what it felt like to be different." I gazed at the people around me, but my eyes stopped on Lando. "He knew what it felt like to be made fun of. To be hurt." Lando's eyebrows drew together, and he looked like he was concentrating on something. Not crying? I looked away from him. "I think sometimes the chickens bullied him." Everyone giggled a little bit. "But he was too kind and gentle to retaliate.

"No one could ever take his place." I turned to Denise, who was holding the small box of ashes. Such a small box. He'd been so skinny when he died. I looked at Connor, who had his phone ready to go with a special Llama Parade song.

"We will miss you forever, Spaghetti," I said. Connor played the song as Denise wiped at her eyes and opened the small box. She shook it into the air. We watched the big ash cloud drift up into the sky, swirling around like it was dancing to the music. But then a breeze picked it up and started blowing the ashes back at us, forcing us all to run down the side of the hill screaming, trying to avoid getting covered in dead llama ashes.

I guess we all took a little piece of Spaghetti home with us that day.

Can you believe in yourself?
Please don't lie.
Can you do it for you?
Tell me you'll try.

—Kids from Alcatraz

MOM AND I WALKED INTO HENRY'S
hospital room together. He looked over from his bed
and gave us a weak half smile. Mom and I sat down next
to his bed, and Mom grabbed his hand. "How are you
feeling today, Henry?"

"Oh," he said, his voice shaky and slurred. "I've been
better."

"Well, you had a minor stroke." Mom squeezed his
hand in both of hers. "It's going to be a bit before you're
feeling yourself."

Henry shook his head. "I think those days are over."

Mom rubbed her hand over his messy, thin, white
hair. "Well, no one knows what might happen." She

turned to me. "Should I go get us some drinks from the cafeteria?"

I nodded, and once she was gone, I moved over a seat so I was closer to Henry. He mumbled something, and I leaned in closer. "What, Henry?"

He mumbled it again, and I had to lean in closer, my face only inches from his. "How many boyfriends do you have, little Aven?" he said, his voice slow and tired.

I sat back and thought about Lando. "None," I told him. "And they're not breaking down my door, if that was going to be your next question."

"They will," Henry said.

"No, I don't think so."

Then Henry turned his face slowly until he was looking right at me. And I could tell he was wasn't just looking at me, but he could clearly see me. He knew me. And he was . . . *angry* with me. "Stop that," he scolded.

I had a hard time meeting his gaze, and I dropped my eyes to the white sheets. "Sorry."

"Stop that, too."

I swallowed and focused on the sheets.

He touched my chin lightly and turned my face to him. "Will you please do something for me?" he said.

I nodded. "Sure."

His lips trembled, and a tear fell down his wrinkled

slack cheek. "Don't ever let anyone make you feel like you're not enough."

"Henry—" I started to say but he shushed me.

"Don't ever let anyone make you think you're not good enough or smart enough or talented enough or brave enough. I let people make me feel that way. They hurt me. They wounded me. On the outside. On the inside. I carried that hurt with me my whole life. I never had anyone around to tell me that even my insignificant life was worth something. But you have so many people who love you and believe in you. And you are worth more than you know. Don't let any one person take that away."

I sniffed. "You need to stop talking like you're going to die. You're going to be all right."

His pale gray eyes watered and spilled over onto his sagging cheeks. "You are good and smart and talented and brave. You have to believe it. Can you do that for me? Can you believe it?"

I wasn't sure if I could do that, but I wouldn't tell Henry no. Not right now. "Yes," I said. "I'll try."

Henry shook his head. "Don't try. Just believe."

I closed my eyes and leaned my cheek into his hand. "Okay," I whispered. "I'll believe." I opened my eyes. "Now I want you to do something for me."

• • •

"Down," I ordered Chili, and she lowered to the ground. I swung my leg over her and slipped my boots into the stirrups. "Stand."

Chili and I walked around the arena a few times, Bill standing at the center watching us. I pulled on the left rein and pushed on Chili's right side with my leg. When we were near Bill, I said, "*Whoa*," and Chili stopped.

I sat on Chili a moment, thinking about Henry's words. *Don't try. Just believe.*

I looked down at Bill. "I'm ready."

His face exploded with excitement. "Really?"

I nodded. "Yes, let's do it before I lose my nerve."

I turned Chili until we faced the jump. "Walk," I told her. I clucked my tongue to move her up a gait, and then we were trotting. I clucked my tongue again to put her at a canter, but as the jump neared, my mind went blank. What was I supposed to do? I couldn't think. In my confusion, I clucked my tongue again, and then Chili was running, and I could hear Bill yelling at us. I'd never run before. No way could I hold on.

And then we were in the air. And then *I* was in the air. By myself. Like, not on the horse anymore. And then I was on the ground. And then the world started fading to black. But before it went completely dark, my final thoughts were that this was how I would die. Just like my birth mother.

I guess I kind of lost my way.
But I'll find it again.
And I'll find it today.

—Kids from Alcatraz

OKAY, SO I TOTALLY DIDN'T DIE.

I can be a tad dramatic at times. I woke up, still lying on the dirt, four worried faces hovering over mine—Mom, Dad, Bill, and Chili.

"Hello?" I said. I wasn't sure what was happening.

"It's okay, Aven," Bill said. "You fell."

"Fell? Off the building?" I definitely wasn't *with it*, as Dad would say.

Mom and Dad exchanged worried looks. "No, Sheebs," Dad said. "You fell off your horse."

"Oh." Things were coming back to me. "Did I do the jump?"

Bill scratched at his beard. "Well, I'd say you did about *half* the jump."

Mom turned to Bill. "Should we try to get her up? Should we take her helmet off?"

"Does anything hurt?" Bill asked.

"My head."

Bill removed his cowboy hat and fanned it lightly at my face. "She might have a concussion."

"But she's wearing a helmet," Dad said.

"She hit the ground hard. A helmet will keep her skull from getting cracked, but it can't stop a concussion. The brain still gets a pretty good jolt. You better get her to the doctor."

I looked from Mom to Dad. "So I fell off the horse?"

Mom rubbed a hand over my cheek. "Yes, honey."

"And I'm not dead?"

"No, sweetheart," Mom said. "You're very much not dead."

"Oh." I smiled a little bit to myself.

"We better get her to the doctor quickly," Mom said. "She's acting funny."

But I was just realizing that the worst thing I feared had happened—I had jumped. I had fallen. I had hit my head. Even gotten knocked unconscious. But I had survived. Which meant I could survive anything.

* * *

The doctor shined a light in my eyes, asked me to follow his finger, moved my head around to check my neck, asked me a bunch of questions about how vomity I felt, and then determined that yes, I did have a concussion.

But I wasn't dead. So I wasn't all that concerned.

Mom and Dad took me out for dinner after the doctor visit. We sat in a dimly lit booth and ordered burgers, though when mine came I felt too nauseated to eat it.

"We'll save it for later, Sheebs," Dad said. "Just drink some water."

Maybe it was the concussion or Henry or Lando. I didn't know. But I sat there in the booth with my parents and vomited everything up. And I don't mean food. I word-vomited everything, *everything*, up. Everything that had happened since the first day of high school—my Great Humiliation, the ongoing bullying, my jealousy over Amanda, and what had happened with Lando.

When at last I was done word-vomiting probably an hour later, and their burgers had gotten cold, they sat there quietly staring down at the table. Mom wiped at her cheeks, then put an arm around me. "Thank you for telling us what's been going on with you."

Dad stared at me from across the booth. "I'd like to kick that Joshua's a—"

"Ben," Mom cut him off. "That won't help. And Aven is solving her own problems like she's always done. Aren't you, honey?"

I nodded. "I'm trying to." I took in a deep breath. "High school has thrown me out of whack. But I'll be okay. I'm sure I will."

"You will," Mom said. "And now you have a few days at home to recover before you have to go back."

"I'm not afraid to go to school anymore," I told her. "And I absolutely have to be back by Halloween."

37

Let's live like we mean it
Because today is the youngest we'll ever be
For the rest of our lives.

—Kids from Alcatraz

I WAS LYING ON MY BED READING *Love, Stargirl*, listening to Llama Parade, trying not to think about Spaghetti, actively recovering from my concussion, when my computer made the little noise that lets me know an email has come in.

I put my eReader down and sat at my desk. I saw who the email was from and nervously clicked on it. I read it. I read it again. I read it a third time. I sat there for a few minutes, thinking. Pondering. My heart racing. I got up, dug my phone out of my bag, and set it on the floor in front of me. I dialed the number from the email with my shaking toe.

A man answered the phone. "Hello," I said to the

man. "My name is Aven Green. I found you on Find My Family."

"This is incredible, Aven," Mom said from the front seat of the car. "I didn't think anything would actually come back from the test. I can't believe it." She sniffled and wiped her eyes.

"When do we meet him, Sheebs?" Dad asked.

"He flies in in a couple of days," I said from the back.

"And he's excited?"

I smiled at him in the rearview mirror. "*So* excited."

Mom took a tissue out of her purse and blew her nose. "Well, he should be. It's simply incredible," she said, her voice cracking. "And to think . . . all these years and he never even knew." She cried into her tissue.

"Are you okay, Mom?"

"I have every right to be emotional right now."

"Well, you'd better get it together," Dad said. "Who knows what might happen at this thing?" He looked at me again in the rearview mirror. "Are we really doing this tonight? Is it too late to back out?"

"Way too late," I said.

Mom dabbed at her eyes with the tissue. "I think it will be fun."

"It's going to be so much fun," I assured them.

"I don't know. . . . " Dad said.

"Remember," I told him. "Today is the youngest you'll ever be for the rest of your life. Do it while you can."

Mom whipped around in her seat and faced me, her eyes huge in the dark car. "Aven, that was *profound*."

"I totally know!" I cried. "It *felt* profound as I was saying it. Like it should be in song or something."

"Hey, remember when you used to write songs?" Dad said.

"Yeah, but they weren't any good."

"They were, too," Mom said. "I think you should try it again."

Dad pulled our little car into a crowded parking lot lit by a few dim street lights. As soon as I stepped out of the car, I could feel the hum of electric guitars shooting across the cool night air. The steady beat of drums pulsed through my whole body.

"Are we sure this is a good idea for Ms. Head Bonk here?" Dad asked, getting out of the car. "I don't know if a loud rock 'n roll concert is the best remedy for a concussion."

"Don't say rock 'n roll," I told him. "It makes you sound old."

"What should I call it then?"

"Punk. And don't worry. I'll stay out of the mosh pit." *This time*, I added secretly to myself.

"What's a mosh pit?" Mom asked as we walked through the parking lot.

"It's like an area where everyone jumps around and slams into one another."

"Yeah, you definitely need to stay out of that," Mom said, then she turned to Dad. "I might try it out, though."

Dad laughed. "Yeah, right, Laura. I can see you now." He shook his head. "Not in a million years."

Mom's face hardened. She stared straight ahead at the big gray block building in front of us, her jaw set with determination. "I am *definitely* going in that mosh pit. Make sure you have your phone out to record me so there's proof."

"This is going to be so much fun," I said. "Thank you guys for taking me."

Dad put an arm around me. "If it's important to you, Sheebs, it's important to us."

"Next stop!" I announced. "The tattoo parlor!"

"No," Mom and Dad both said immediately.

I sighed. "Yes, I suppose there is a limit to your coolness."

"You'll rethink that statement when you see me moshing," Mom said. "Or is it mosh-pitting?"

I laughed. "Moshing."

Trilby and her parents were standing outside the building already waiting for us. Trilby threw her arms around me. "I'm so happy you're here!" she cried.

She pulled away, and my mouth dropped open. She ran a hand over her shaved head, which had hair chalk designs all over it—flowers and rainbows mostly. "Oh, yeah," she said. "What do you think?"

"I think you look incredible. But why did you do it? Is it because of the heat?"

"I decided my hair was just another way I was conforming to the Man's expectations of me," she said. "And it feels amazing!" She rubbed her hands frantically over her head and jumped around in a circle. "And think of all the money I'll save on shampoo!"

I tore my eyes away from Trilby's scalp and found Mom and Dad were already chatting with her parents—wanting to know how things were going with the smoothie shop, how they liked working at Stagecoach Pass. Dad eventually asked what to expect from "this thing."

Trilby's mom put a hand on Dad's shoulder. "Don't worry, Ben—no crowd-surfing for first-timers. And Screaming Ferret's a good intro to punk. Nothing too hardcore."

"I'm actually going to go in there and listen to something called Screaming Ferret?" Dad said. "Do they think that name makes them sound enjoyable?"

"Dad!" I cried. "You're going to like them. They're amazing!"

I loved the sound of the music blasting through the small opened doorway as we waited in line to pay cover charges and get our hands stamped. The bouncer took one look at Trilby then told her to put her hand out. He stamped "underage" on it. "No going into the over twenty-one area for you, baldie," the bouncer said. Then he turned his attention to me. He scanned over me, an intense look of contemplation on his face. He scratched at his tattooed neck. Then he stamped "underage" on my nub.

The bouncer gave our parents wristbands (and I thought Mom was going to die of pride when he asked for her ID), and then let us into the stuffy, loud, crowded building.

We slowly inched our way closer and closer to the stage, completely surrounded by singing, dancing, and shouting people—most of them older than Trilby and me but definitely younger than our parents. Our group didn't exactly fit the punk-show profile. And I loved that.

We all stopped when we reached a small open area surrounding the mosh pit. It was pure chaos in there—people flying here and there and everywhere. Every now and then someone would tumble out of the pit and into the crowd and the crowd would push them back in. I'd never felt so much energy in my life.

"Get ready to record, Ben!" Mom cried out, but Dad just stood there gaping at Mom as she flung herself into the mosh pit.

"You shouldn't have told her she wouldn't do it!" I shouted in his ear.

He laughed and pulled out his phone to record her. A young guy with about a dozen piercings in his face stuck his hand up at Mom and cried out, "Right on, lady!" Mom smacked his hand before someone slammed into her, knocking her out of our sight and into the chaos. Dad kept recording, even though we couldn't see Mom anymore. I guessed he was hoping she would come up for air at some point and he could catch another glimpse of her. I realized right then in that moment that Dad didn't just love Mom. He *liked* her, liked her. And he liked her. That was maybe the most important thing of all.

I stood there awhile, taking in the scene, gazing around at all the people, all dressed so differently, like we were at Comic Con again, and they were wearing costumes.

But they weren't wearing costumes at all. And the people at Comic Con weren't wearing costumes. Lando as Captain America—Isaiah Bradley—jumping up on the coffee table and flexing his foamy muscles—that was the real Lando. Lando at school was the Lando in costume. I looked next to me at Trilby, at her shaved head with the colorful designs, at her tank top with another punk band on it. Trilby *never* wore a costume. I watched as she pumped her fist in the air, jumped up and down, and sang along to the music. She stopped and looked at me, breathing hard, sweat already pouring down her face. "Who cares, Aven?" she yelled. "Just who the heck cares?"

I closed my eyes, let the music, the lyrics fully sink in.

I'm seeing things clearly now
For the first time ever.
I see me.
I'm not what they thought.
I am what I believe.

I found myself yelling the words along with Trilby as she put her arm around my shoulder. And then we were jumping up and down together, shouting and singing and fighting in our own tiny way against the Man.

And I finally knew exactly who the Man was in my life.

The Man was Joshua and his friends.

The Man was Janessa looking at me like she was better than me.

The Man was every kid who'd ever called me a freak.

The Man was movies and magazines and books that portrayed beauty as being only one thing.

The Man was every single person who had ever seen me as *less than*.

The Man in my life was sometimes . . . me.

I opened my eyes and looked at Trilby. She stopped jumping and raised her eyebrows at me. "Thank you," I yelled at her.

She smiled. "You're welcome," she screamed.

Sometimes the friends you make aren't the ones you expected. And sometimes the place you find yourself in isn't the place you were hoping for. And sometimes, if you keep an open mind, you'll find they're so much better than what you imagined.

No action means no results.
Get up. Get moving. Get out of your seat.
Fight, fight, fight.
You can take the heat.

—Screaming Ferret

ZION STARED ACROSS OUR LUNCH
table at me. "You look good."

"Shut up," I said.

"No, really. My mom did a great job of fitting—"

"I swear I will Kung Fu your face if you say another
word."

Zion stuck a carrot stick in his mouth, loudly
chewed it, and swallowed. "I don't think you're using
that word right."

"I don't care."

"Just saying—I'm pretty sure it's not a verb."

"Just saying—I don't care."

Zion took another bite of carrot. "You want to go trick or treating later?"

"Aren't we getting too old?"

Zion frowned. "Are we?"

I stared at him. "I don't know. Aren't we?"

"I don't know . . . Are we?"

I shrugged. "Nah, let's go. We can do your neighborhood."

"Well, we can't exactly trick or treat at Stagecoach Pass."

Just then, with the greatest flourish I had ever seen, Lando burst through the cafeteria doors, all giant foamy muscles and blue and red spandex and plastic wings on his masked head.

He ran through the cafeteria, a blur of blue, stopping every few seconds to put his hand over his brow and scan the room. Several kids giggled as they watched him.

My heart pounded as I hunched down in my seat, wishing I could pull my green robe over my head. Zion glared at me. "Scaredy cat." I sat back up straight and turned to Lando. He spotted me and his mouth opened wide. Then he jumped up on the nearest table and pointed at me. "You dare come here to challenge me, Armless Master!" His voice boomed through the cafeteria, which was quiet now except for some snorts and giggles.

I shakily stood up from my seat and faced him.

I am Aven Green.

I am good.

I am brave.

I am punk.

And I am fighting the Man with every action I make.

"I do," I said, my voice not nearly as strong as Lando's.

He jumped down from the table and walked dramatically to me, whipping his head around. I bit my quivering lip. He pushed his foamy-muscled chest into my foamy-muscled chest and we bounced off of each other. "So, we meet again, Armless Master."

"So we do," I said, wishing I had some better comeback, wishing I were capable of mustering something even slightly witty at that moment.

"At last I have found the secret weapon to defeat you! You SHAN'T survive!"

I giggled, my face so blazing hot at this point, it could fry bacon. "Do your worst."

Lando threw an arm around my waist and pulled me to him. He leaned in and whispered hesitantly, "Can I kiss you?"

The last time I thought a boy was going to kiss me flashed into my mind, and my fear and insecurity from the past several weeks tried once more to take over, to control me.

But I wouldn't let it.

Because this was nothing like that time. And Lando was nothing like that boy. And I was already stronger than that girl.

I nodded and closed my eyes. Trusting. Again.

It felt good to trust.

Then he pressed his lips to mine.

Firm.

Soft.

Warm.

Cool.

It was pretty much everything I'd ever hoped it would be, even when I pretended that I'd never hoped for it all.

Lando pulled back with a loud dramatic smack.

Of all the ways I had imagined my first kiss to happen, this was certainly not one of them. It wasn't private. It wasn't tender. It wasn't like in some romantic comedy or fairy tale. And I doubted anyone's first kiss was like mine. Like everything else in my life, it had to be totally and completely weird, funny, bizarre, and different.

Lando pranced away from me like a ballerina,

jumping through the air, one arm outstretched like he was on a serious mission. Real Lando had crashed into School Lando. And I was glad to see it.

Lando turned as he reached the cafeteria doors. "This isn't over, Armless Master!" He raised a finger in the air. "It shall never be over between us! NEVAH!" Then he burst out of the cafeteria.

Everything went completely back to the way it was. The sounds of noisy high schoolers resumed as though nothing had happened, and I sat back down across from Zion. He took another bite of carrot and sighed. "That was so unrealistic. Captain America and the Armless Master aren't even in the same comic book universe."

I shook my head, my brain buzzing, my pulse still rapid, my feet bouncing on the cafeteria floor. "You truly are a geek."

Zion's lip turned up a little at one corner, and I think I glimpsed a hint of pride in his brown eyes at my words.

I snuck a glance at Lando's table. He hadn't come back, but two girls sitting there were watching me. The moment I made eye contact with them, they smiled. Then they *waved*. I smiled and lifted my foot to wave back at them. They giggled and waved again.

I guess everything hadn't gone *completely* back to the way it was.

39

We meet again.
My old friend.
Together till the end.

—Kids from Alcatraz

I WALKED INTO THE HOSPITAL
room. I sat down next to Henry's bed. He turned his
head to me. "Hello," he said.

I sincerely hoped he was clear today. "Hi, Henry," I
said. "Do you know who I am?"

He smiled. "Aven."

"Aven Green," I said.

He nodded. "Aven Green."

"I'm doing it, Henry," I told him. "I'm taking your
advice."

He licked his shaking wrinkled lips. "I'm glad."

"I have something important to tell you," I said,
hardly able to keep my voice steady.

His face lit up. "What is it?"

"Well, um, there's someone here to see you."

"Who? Joe?"

"No, Joe was here earlier. Remember?"

He nodded. "Oh yeah."

"She'll be back tomorrow. There's someone else here to see you."

"Who?"

"Just a second." I got up and went out into the hallway. I came back with a man pushing an older man in a wheelchair. I sat back down at Henry's bedside.

"Who are they?" Henry asked.

"This is Robert," I said. "And this is his father, Walter." Both men seemed like they were straining hard not to cry as they watched Henry. "They came all the way from Chicago to see you."

"To see me?" Henry said.

I nodded. "Henry . . ." I swallowed hard. And swallowed again. "Walter is your brother." Henry's mouth dropped open as he stared at the two men. "He's been searching for you his whole life."

I moved out of the way, and Robert pushed Walter to Henry's bedside. Henry's mouth opened and closed, opened and closed. His lips trembled. He pushed the button on his bed so he could sit all the way up and face his brother.

They looked so much alike. It was like Henry was looking into a mirror—a mirror that made him look even older than his already really old self.

Walter stuck out a feeble, shaking hand, and Henry grasped it. They stared at each other, holding hands, little gasps escaping their mouths, sniffing every now and then, until Walter said in a hoarse, whisper-like voice, "I was five when Mama and Daddy died. You were only a baby. I wanted to take care of you, but they took you away from me. You and Nora. She was only three."

"Nora?" Henry said.

"She was our sister," Walter said. "I don't know where she is. I haven't been able to find her. I thought you both might be dead. But here you are."

"You've been looking for me?" Henry said.

"All my life."

And then they sat crying together for a long time. There was a lot of lost time to cry for.

Stay beside me,
And I won't hide me.
With you to guide me,
I'll finally find me.

—Kids from Alcatraz

CONNOR PUT THE HELIUM BALLOON
to his mouth and sucked in a deep breath. "How do I
sound?" he asked in a high-pitched voice.

"Like a munchkin," I said, attempting to put a balloon over the helium nozzle with my foot.

Connor barked and we burst out laughing. "Now
you sound like a poufy little Pomeranian," I said.

"Do you need help, Aven?" Amanda asked.

I shook my head. "Nope." I was sitting up on the
table in the steakhouse, one foot on a chair, the other
one straining to get the balloon on the helium nozzle. It slid on at last, and I pushed the rubber nozzle
down with my foot. *"Aha!"* I cried, but when I tried to

remove the helium-filled balloon, it went flying off the nozzle and blew around the room, making loud farting noises.

Amanda took a new balloon and filled it on the helium tank. Then she smiled and held it out to my mouth. I stared at her a moment. She blinked her left eye and jerked her head a little. I leaned forward and opened my mouth. I sucked in a breath. "So Amanda," I said in my high-pitched voice. "I heard you play the piano."

She giggled. "Yeah. And I heard you play the guitar. It's pretty cool that you can play with your feet."

"Yep. Maybe we should start a band." I motioned my head at Zion, who was busy dropping napkins and forks onto tables. "Zion over there is getting pretty good on the guitar, but Connor's a huge slacker."

Connor shrugged. "I think I'm more a drum guy."

"That's good," I said. "Because we need one in our band." Amanda and I smiled at each other. Darn it. I liked her a lot, and I could see why Connor did, too.

Trilby and her parents walked in then. "Trilby definitely has to join our band," I said loud enough for her to hear.

She bounded over to us, her eyes huge. "You guys are starting a band?"

"Yeah, we just need a lead singer."

Trilby wasted no time; she ran up the steps to the stage, pulled the microphone off its stand, and started wailing out some hardcore punk song.

We all clapped and cheered when she was done. "How did I do?" she asked, rejoining our group.

"You're our new lead singer."

Trilby spun around in a circle. "Man, I always wanted to be in a punk band."

Amanda's eyes were huge. "It's a punk band? I mean, do punk bands usually have piano players in them?"

"I can't think of any," Trilby said. Then she raised her fists in the air and shook them. "We'll be so original!"

"What about our name?" Connor said.

I thought a moment. "How about The Outcasts?"

Trilby shook her head. "Nah. We need something more unique."

I gazed up at Lando, who was standing on a ladder hanging streamers from a chandelier made out of antlers. He looked down at me and smiled. "You want to join our band?" I called up to him.

"Heck, yeah. What kind of band?"

"Punk band."

"What can I do?"

I grinned. "You can be our groupie."

Zion put a hand over his mouth to stifle a laugh, but Lando glared at him. "I'm going to learn guitar faster than that guy down there, and then we'll see who's the groupie."

"The guys from Screaming Ferret learned how to play a few chords on the guitar and were recording songs *that same day*," Trilby said.

"Well, then we're way ahead of them," Lando said. "Because Aven already plays like a boss."

I smiled up at him. "If you join us, we can call our band Alcatraz," I told him.

"Oh, I like it," Trilby said. "But why Alcatraz?"

"Amanda, Lando, Connor, Trilby, Aven, and Zion. Get it? Alcatraz."

"Oh," Trilby said. "I thought maybe it was because we would help people escape from the Alcatraz of their minds as a result of the expectations society has placed on them by using the power of our glorious punk rock melodies!"

"Yeah, that too," I said.

Connor had his phone out. "Nope," he said. "Already exists." He cringed. "And I'm not sure I want to be confused for these other bands."

I thought a moment. "Then how about Kids from Alcatraz?"

"Yes!" Trilby cried. "Because we've all escaped from the prison of the establishment into the freedom of the punk world!"

I laughed. "I don't think you've ever been imprisoned, Trilby."

Amanda knotted a balloon. "So this is a welcome home party?"

"Yeah," I said. "And also a farewell party."

Amanda tied a ribbon around the balloon and let it soar up to the ceiling. "Who's the welcome home party for?"

"Henry."

"And who's the farewell party for?"

I sighed. "Henry."

Mom walked in carrying a giant tray of hamburger buns. "Who wants to bring in the fixings?" she asked.

Lando jumped down from the ladder. "I will."

Dad put a giant bowl of coleslaw down on a table, and Connor and I looked at each other. We burst out laughing.

"What's so funny?" Amanda asked.

Connor shrugged. "Inside joke."

Amanda's face fell. "I'll tell you guys the story later," I said to her and Trilby. "We don't want to spoil your appetite right now."

"Hey, Mom," I said as she pulled buns out of bags and placed them on plates. "We're starting a punk band. Since you won't let me tat up my nubs, you have to at least let me pierce my nose."

She and Dad looked at each other and grinned. "We'll think about it," Mom said.

"Yes!" I cried, and if I had a fist I definitely would have been pumping it.

Then Dad whispered something to Mom and she left the steakhouse just as Josephine walked in with Milford. He gave me a little hug then shuffled over to help Zion with the utensils.

I raised an eyebrow at Josephine, but she shook her head at me. "Don't start with me, little girl."

"You have a boyfriend."

"I most certainly do not."

"Josephine and Milford sitting in a tree, K-I—"

"Knock it off."

"S-S-I-N-G," I finished quickly. "Are you seriously going to give me a grandpa named Milford?"

She rolled her eyes.

"Grandma Joe and Grandpa Milford," I teased her. The annoyed look left her face and she stared at me. "What?" I asked.

She pursed her lips. "Nothing." Her eyes got all glassy.

"Oh my gosh. What is it?"

She shook her head and blinked. "Nothing, You . . . you never called me that before."

"Oh," I said. "Well, don't get used to it."

She waved a hand in the air. "Gracious, no. I feel old enough without having to be called Grandma."

I smiled at her. She patted my shoulder awkwardly and walked off to talk to Denise, who was busy mixing lemonade. I found Dad on the stage where we sometimes had amateurish country bands play during dinner. He was messing with the sound system. "I heard you're the DJ for tonight."

"That's me."

"You better not play any of that terrible folk music you like. This place will clear out like someone dropped a stink bomb in it."

He narrowed his eyes at me. "Are you comparing the beautiful melodies of Bob Dylan to a stink bomb?"

"His voice sure sounds like a stink bomb."

"I didn't know a stink bomb had sound," Dad said, unraveling a knotted-up cord. "I thought it just had stink." He looked up. "Oh, he's here."

I turned and saw Robert pushing Henry in his wheelchair into the dining area.

"Surprise!" we all called out.

He smiled and clapped his hands weakly. "What's all this?"

"Surprise party for you, Henry," Mom said. "To show you how glad we are to have you back."

A woman entered the dining room pushing Henry's brother in his wheelchair. Walter introduced her to me as his daughter-in-law. Everyone was so excited to meet Walter and hear his stories about his long search for his little brother.

When I finally had Henry to myself, I knelt down in front of his wheelchair. "Hi, Henry," I said.

He gave me a shaky smile. "Hi, little Aven."

"Henry." I swallowed. "This isn't just a welcome home party for you. It's a goodbye party, too."

Henry's smiled disappeared. "Goodbye?"

I blinked. "Don't you think it's time for you to retire?"

His smile returned. "Yes, I think I'm ready to retire. But I'll still be around."

I looked over at Walter and his son and daughter-in-law. They all had big smiles as they talked to everyone gathered around them. The crowd burst out laughing at something Walter said. I turned back to Henry. "They want to take you home with them. Home to Chicago. They want to take care of you."

Henry shook his head. "I can't go to Chicago. I live here."

"But they're you're family, Henry. Don't you want to go be with your family?"

"They're very nice people. And I'm so grateful you found them for me. But they're strangers." Then he held a finger out. I followed it with my eyes to see what he was pointing at: Josephine. "There's my family," Henry said. Then he pointed at Mom. "There's my family." Then at Dad and Denise and the other Stagecoach Pass workers. "There's my family." He looked down at me and touched a hand to my cheek. "There's my family." He smiled. "Family is about a lot more than blood. You should know that better than anyone, Aven." He patted my cheek. "I have to stay here."

I *should* know that better than anyone. Why did I feel like I still had so much to learn? "Okay," I whispered. I stood up.

"Josephine says the food at Golden Sunset's pretty good," Henry said. "She said they have Steak Diane."

I smiled. "You'll like it there. And I'll come visit all the time."

He nodded. "Now that sounds like a pretty good deal."

I saw Mom watching me from where she sat at a

table, a large wrapped gift in front of her. I walked over and sat down next to her. I could see her staring at me in my peripheral vision. I turned my head. "What?"

"Nothing."

"What is it?"

"You always find new ways to surprise me. That's all."

"Are you upset I used the kit on Henry?"

"No. No, not upset. Just surprised. I thought you wanted to find your father."

I gazed at the stage. He'd finally untangled the wires and had gotten the music on. "There he is," I said. "He's right over there, playing that awful music." I stood up and shouted, "Play something else!" I watched as Lando walked over and talked to Dad for a minute, then Dad put on a way better song.

I looked at the present in front of Mom. "Is that for Henry?"

She pushed it to me. "No, it's for you."

"For me?"

"We never got you anything to celebrate the start of high school."

"Well, it didn't feel like something worth celebrating." I smiled. "Until now."

"We were going to save it for Christmas, but this felt like the right time." She raised an eyebrow. "Since you're starting a punk band and all. What's the name of your band by the way?"

"Kids from Alcatraz." I tore open the wrapping paper with my feet and unzipped the black canvas case.

"Is that yours?" Trilby squealed from behind me.

I nodded, not able to take my eyes off my gift.

"It's amazing!" she said. "It's perfect for Kids from Alcatraz."

Zion walked up to admire my brand new sea-foam green electric guitar. Or at least pretend he was admiring my electric guitar. "Wow, it's so cool." He shuffled from foot to foot. "I know how much you like to dance." He said softly, looking at the guitar instead of Trilby.

"You talking to me?" she said.

He nodded.

She laughed and grabbed his hand, dragging him onto the dance floor, where Josephine and Milford were already dancing together.

Lando came over and picked up my new guitar. "You are going to rock with this, Aven."

Mom smiled. "Yeah, she will."

He put it back down on the table. "So are you going to dance with me this time if I ask you?"

I looked up at him. "I've never danced, you know, like that before. I don't know how."

Lando shrugged. "There's not much to it. You can just go like this." He swayed lazily from side to side.

I giggled. "Okay. That looks easy enough."

I walked with Lando to the dance floor. I held my breath as he put his arms around my waist. And then we swayed like he'd shown me.

"I've been wanting to tell you something," I said.

"What?"

"I loved your drawings."

Lando's face lit up. "Really?"

"Yeah. I mean, Zion told me you liked to draw, but I had no idea. You're very talented. Your art . . . it's amazing. It . . . " I glanced down at our feet. It was difficult to make eye contact in such close proximity to someone, and I wasn't used to being this close. "It looked just like me. But not just like me on the outside. It looked like me on the inside, too."

"Well," Lando swayed from foot to foot, "that's the part I like the best."

I cleared my throat and willed my cheeks not to get too bright pink. "Does she have a name?" I asked.

"Still working on that," Lando said. "I was thinking of *The Great Green, Defender of Nerds.*"

I giggled. "And what's her superpower? I mean besides using her feet like her hands and defending nerds."

"She can do anything she wants," Lando said. "And she never cares what anyone else thinks about it."

I looked down, my cheeks blazing hot. "So is this seriously it?" I asked him. "I mean dancing?"

"I could dip you."

I shook my head. "Oh, no. No, no, no. No dipping."

"Why not?"

"I can't hang on to you. I might fall."

"Look at it like a trust exercise," he said. "Like when someone falls back and has to trust someone will catch them."

"I know what a trust exercise is."

"Well," Lando raised an eyebrow, "don't you trust me?"

I closed my eyes, my heart beating rapidly. "I do."

And then I was falling backward, terrified of crashing into the gross steakhouse dance floor and possibly getting another concussion and greasy peanut shells and sawdust in my hair, but Lando pulled me back up before that could happen.

"See?" He pushed my hair away from my face. "I didn't drop you."

I breathed heavily as my heart slowed down. "You didn't."

Connor walked up. "She's never danced with me before," he said.

Lando stepped away. "Go ahead."

I watched as Lando went over to Amanda and started talking to her.

"Well?" Connor said. "Are you going to dance with me?"

"You kind of have to make the first move."

He put his arms around my waist like Lando had. I stared at my friend. My best friend. "So is Lando your boyfriend now?" he asked.

I shrugged. "I don't know. I don't know how this all works. Is Amanda your girlfriend?"

He shook his head and clucked his tongue. "Nah. She's just a friend." He cleared his throat. "Would you get mad if I told you something?"

"What?"

"I think," Connor blinked his eyes rapidly, "if you told me Lando was your boyfriend, I think I would be jealous." His cheeks reddened, and he barked.

"Can I tell you something?" I asked

He nodded without looking at me.

"I'm kind of jealous of Amanda. I was worried you replaced me."

His lip turned up a little. "I could never replace you."

"And I could never replace you."

I realized then that when you truly cared about

someone, it didn't matter how far apart you lived. You would still make the effort to be friends. Because real friends were worth all the effort in the world. "I'm glad we're still friends."

"We'll always be friends," Connor said.

"Best friends."

The song ended, and Dad put on a new one. I groaned. "Really, Dad?" I said and Connor laughed.

I walked to the stage and glared at him, tapping my foot. "Oh, fine," he said. "Do you have a request, my sweet loving daughter? What melodious punk song would you like me to play?"

"I do have a request," I told him. "But it's not a punk song."

**It's not always easy to find the good.
But it's in there somewhere.
You'll find it if you would.**

—Kids from Alcatraz

I SAT AT MY DESK THE NEXT DAY,
listening to the sounds of the player piano below me.
"The Entertainer" song didn't sound quite so annoying
today. I typed out a new blog post:

> Okay, so high school got off to a rough start for
> me. Like, a seriously rough start—as rough as
> sandpaper made out of cactuses and pine cones.
> And porcupines. But things are looking up. I'm
> trying to go back to seeing the positives in life.
> And for the first time since everything went wrong,
> I think I can do this. I can make it. I'll survive. After

all, there are actually some good things about starting high school. Here are twenty:

1.　Three thousand kids. Three thousand potential new friends.

2.　Comic Con. Comic Con was pretty cool. I'll definitely give it another try next year, though I don't think I'll go as Armless Master again. Arm-Fall-Off-Boy is a possibility, though. And then I would have some arm weapons to battle with if anyone messed with me. (I'm looking at you, Wolverine!)

3.　Football games. Especially when one of the players is super-cool. And super-cute.

4.　Bullies getting the justice they deserve. Okay, I know that sounds vengeful and I should remove it from my list. Consider it removed.

5.　Algebra. Because I can always tackle math.

6.　Wearing a terrible costume to school for Halloween and not caring what other people think.

7.   I've decided to add back "Bullies getting the justice they deserve."

8.   Zombie tarantulas coming back from the dead with new legs. Turns out Fathead was just molting.

9.   The look on Zion's face when I stuck Fathead's molted exoskeleton on the lunch table.

10. Seeing long-lost family members reunited, especially when it was never their choice to be apart.

11. Horseback riding.

12. First crushes.

13. First kisses.

14. Pretzels are X9 in the vending machine. I can reach X9. And I'm getting taller. The Cheetos will soon be mine. Oh, yes. They will be mine.

15. I'm not only getting taller, but also I think I might be getting wiser. And part of that wisdom is

no longer feeling ashamed because of something someone else has done that has nothing to do with me and everything to do with them.

16. Going to my first punk show, though Mom did leave with a black eye. She wore it proudly like it was an Olympic medal.

17. Friends who embarrass themselves in public for you.

18. Friends who risk everything to defend you.

19. Friends who lie down on their backs in the middle of a greasy steakhouse dance floor to do the "Y.M.C.A." with their feet for you.

20. Friends who see the real you, even when you can't.

No one could ever take your place, Spaghetti.
We love you forever, Spaghetti.
Not meatballs, not baked ziti, not even lasagna.
Spaghetti, Spaghetti, Spaghetti.
We love you forever, Spaghetti.

—Kids from Alcatraz
(debut song—five downloads sold)

I MARCHED ACROSS THE DIRT OF MAIN

Street in my riding boots. It was crowded today at Stagecoach Pass   the first crowded day we'd had since the festival.

I walked into the horse stall and laid my head on Chili's side, feeling her breath. I closed my eyes. For the first time ever, I felt like maybe we were in sync. But whether we were in sync enough, I was about to find out.

"Aven?" I looked up and saw Mom and Dad standing outside the stall. "You okay, Sheebs?" Dad asked.

I nodded and smiled. "Yes."

Mom clapped her hands. "We have a surprise for you."

I followed them to the petting zoo, where a handful of kids were brushing the goats. We went into the covered area.

"Oh my gosh!" I cried when I saw the small llama. I knelt down in front of him. Though he only had three legs, he didn't seem to have any trouble standing. "Hey, boy," I said, nuzzling my face into his soft fur. I'd missed the feel of that soft llama fur.

"We got him from a llama rescue," Dad said. "We knew as soon as we saw him he was the one for us."

"Just like we knew when we saw you," Mom said.

I swallowed and kissed the top of his head. "What's his name?" I asked.

Mom and Dad glanced at each other. Then Mom's smile fell. "Mama."

I looked from Mom to Dad and back to Mom. "His name is Mama? Mama the llama?"

Mom shook her head. "The people who run the llama rescue let their three-year-old name the llamas who come in without a name."

I nodded slowly. "Ah, that explains it." I turned my attention back to Mama. "You know, I'm not sure I can

live with the name Mama. I mean, especially considering he's a dude."

Dad grinned. "You can name him anything you
want."

I stared into the llama's deep brown eyes. Ran my
cheek over his soft cream-colored fur. I felt a pang for
Spaghetti. But Spaghetti was gone, and it was time to
let go. Of a lot of things.

"What are you thinking?" Dad asked.

"I'm thinking . . ." I looked up at my parents and
smiled. "Lasagna."

"Connor, Connor, Connor!" I cried when I saw him
walking down Main Street. "I got a new llama! And he
only has three legs! And his name is Lasagna!"

He barked. "Cool."

It was only then that I saw Connor was with a man.
I didn't need anyone to tell me this was Connor's dad—
he had the same hazel eyes and light brown hair as his
son.

"Aven, this is my dad," Connor said.

"Oh."

The man smiled. "Nice to meet you, Aven. Connor's
told me a lot about you."

I raised an eyebrow at Connor. "Really?"

"Yes, really," Connor said.

I looked back at Connor's dad. "It's nice to meet you, Mr. Bradley. Connor's told me a lot about you, too."

Mr. Bradley cringed. "I hope it's not all been bad, even if I deserve it."

I smiled at him. "It's not all been bad."

We walked ahead of Connor's dad, and I whispered to Connor, "What's going on?"

Connor shrugged. "He found out about this, and he wanted to meet you, and he asked if he could take me, so I thought . . . What would Aven do?"

I grinned at him. "And what would Aven do?"

Connor nudged me with his shoulder. "Aven would give him a second chance," he said. "Because Aven always believes the best about people."

I left Connor and his dad at the stands and went into the stall with Chili. I stood in front of her, pure determination. "Are you ready?" I asked her.

She snorted in response.

"Well, I hope that was a yes." I took a deep breath. "Let's do this."

She lowered her head to my foot, but my boot was on. "You can have all the face rubs you want afterward."

Bill walked into the stall holding my helmet. "Are you ready, Aven?" I nodded as he set the helmet on top of my head and buckled it. Then he patted the side of it. "I'm proud of you, you know?"

"You are?"

"Yeah, not everyone has the guts to get back up on a horse after they've had a good fall."

I thought about Bill's words as I walked with Chili out to the arena. I'd had a pretty darn good fall. But I wasn't about to stay down. I would keep getting back up, no matter how many times I fell. And no one could keep me down. *No one.*

We were at the center of the arena now. "Down," I told Chili, ignoring the people in the stands. She lowered, and people *ahhed* over how smart she was. She was a smart girl.

I swung my leg over Chili and slipped my boots into the stirrups. "Stand." Chili stood. I tapped her lightly with my feet. "Walk." We walked around the arena for a moment. "*Whoa,*" I said to her.

For the first time I looked out at the crowd. I saw Connor and his dad. I saw Zion and Lando. I saw Josephine and Milford and Henry and Mom and Dad. I saw Trilby. I saw my friends. I saw my family.

I kicked gently at Chili's sides. "Walk." As we neared the jump, I clucked my tongue. Chili went into a trot, leaving a trail of dust behind us. I clucked my tongue again. Chili moved into a canter. The jump was close now. We were moving fast, the warm fall air of the Arizona desert blowing in my face. I closed my eyes to it. Leaned into it. Embraced it.

Don't try. Just believe.

And then I was in the air again. But I wasn't afraid of falling.

ACKNOWLEDGMENTS

Thank you to my editors, Christina Pulles and Suzy Capozzi. To Heather Kelly for designing an amazing cover, complete with cape. And thank you to everyone else at Sterling for the constant support: Theresa Thompson, Lauren Tambini, Maha Khalil, Chris Vaccari, and the entire sales team. Thank you to my agent, Shannon Hassan. To Barbie Thomas, Tisha Shelton, and all my sensitivity readers. To my favorite writer people: Stephanie Elliott, Kelly Devos, and Lorri Phillips. You three girls are my lifeboat in this choppy publishing sea. Thank you to all the booksellers, librarians, and educators who work so hard to spread book love to children. To my husband for his unwavering belief in me. To Bronte, Adlai, and Monet for always inspiring me. Thank you to God for His endless blessings. And to my readers—I hope you enjoyed spending a bit more time with Aven.

MOMENTOUS EVENTS
IN THE LIFE OF A CACTUS
∘ DISCUSSION QUESTIONS ∘

1 This book is told in the first person, from Aven's point of view. How do you think the story would change if it were told from another character's point of view? Some characters to consider are Zion, Lando, Trilby, Connor, and Joshua.

2 Why do you think the book is titled *Momentous Events in the Life of a Cactus*? What happens in the story that Aven considers momentous?

3 Aven has very diverse interests: horseback riding, guitar, soccer, and now punk music. What are your interests? How do you share your interests with others?

4 Before reading the story, would you have thought that a person without arms could do all of the things that Aven can do? What does that tell you about making assumptions about the capabilities of others?

5 Consider how you talk about people with disabilities. Why do you think it's important to use "person-first" language?

6 How do you react when you see a person with a visible disability? How do you think people with disabilities would want you to react? What makes you feel welcomed when you meet someone?

7 Are disabilities always visible? What kinds of challenges do you think a person with a hidden disability might have?

8 Why do you think Aven is so determined to find out if Henry has any family? What makes people family?

9 Aven discovers a love of punk rock in the story. What do you think it means to be punk rock?

10 What do you think you should do if someone won't stop verbally bullying you or someone else? Do you think Aven handled the situation well? What can you do to be an upstander?

11 Which characters in this book experienced personal growth? How did they change? Were there any characters who didn't appear to grow or change?

12 Did reading this book change your opinions or perspectives on anything? How?

13 It was difficult for Aven to learn how to ride and jump a horse. Is there something in your life you're struggling to learn? What steps can you take to tackle it?

14 Aven has a rough start to high school, but she's able to get through it largely due to supportive friends. How do your friends support you during tough times? How can you support your friends?

15 Connor has to forgive his father in order to start rebuilding their relationship. Can you think of a time in your life when you've had to forgive someone or needed forgiveness from someone? How did forgiveness make you feel?